Other
WACKiLY WONDROUS WORKS
by this author

Vordak the Incomprehensible:
How to Grow Up and Rule the World

Vordak the Incomprehensible:
Rule the School

Vordak the Incomprehensible:
Double Trouble

EGMONT
USA
New York

EGMONT
We bring stories to life
First published by Egmont USA, 2013
443 Park Avenue South, Suite 806
New York, NY 10016

Copyright © Scott Seegert, 2013
Illustrations by John Martin
All rights reserved

1 3 5 7 9 8 6 4 2

www.egmontusa.com
www.vordak.com

Library of Congress Cataloging-in-Publication Data

Seegert, Scott.
  Time travel trouble / by Scott Seegert.
     pages cm. -- (Vordak the Incomprehensible ; #4)
   Summary: In an attempt to finally best his arch-nemesis, Commander Virtue, supervillain
Vordak the Incomprehensible attempts traveling back in time, with disastrous results.
  ISBN 978-1-60684-461-8 (hardcover)
  [1. Supervillains--Fiction. 2. Time travel--Fiction. 3. Humorous stories.] I. Title.
  PZ7.S45157Ti 2013
  [Fic]--dc23
  2012045853

Cover art by John Martin
Cover design by Kathy Westray
Text and page layout by Karen Hudson
Printed in U.S.A.

DEDICATION

This book is dedicated to my arch-nemesis,
Commander Virtue.

(No—not really. But now he'll think we're friends, and when
he comes to my front door with a plate of chocolate chip
cookies, it will be a simple matter to capture him in one of
my Diabolically Clever Yet Extremely Slow-Acting Death
Traps! MUAHAHAHAHA!!!)

ACKNOWLEDGMENTS

Following is a list of all the wonderfully talented individuals
who not only helped make this book possible, but also met
my demand of $5 to include their names:

Irene the Unmerciful-Incomprehensible (Thanks, Mom!)
Regina Griffin—Editor Extraordinaire
Dan Lazar—Agent Acceptable (You still owe me $1.75!)
All the fine folks at Egmont and Writers House (Sorry, but
$5 combined does not get your individual names listed.)

CHAPTER ONE

CONGRATULATIONS, ordinary person! You must be smarter than you look. Why? Because you are, at this very moment, reading the introduction to my latest book. Which means you were able to figure out how to yank on the cover and open it up, hopefully without using your teeth. Which means you *must* be smarter than you look. So, again, congratulations!

You are also incredibly *lucky*. (And not just because you're smarter than you look—although you should certainly be grateful for that.) Do you see this door?

"I don't think so."

You *don't think so*? By the tarnished toenails of Tanzor, it's right there in front of you!

"I mean I don't think I'm smarter than I look."

I must say . . . I'm beginning to agree.

"No. I mean that I think I look like I'm pretty smart to begin with."

MUAHAHAHAHA!!! Oh, stop it, already! My sinister sides are beginning to split! I haven't laughed this hard since . . . oh, wait a minute . . . you weren't kidding, were you? Well, this is awkward. I'll tell you what—if you are an ordinary *male* person, look into the first mirror. If you are an ordinary *female* person, look into the second mirror.

Case closed! Now, as I was about to say—you are incredibly *lucky* because of what lies **beyond** this door.

Right you are! And the reason you are so lucky is that you have the glorious good fortune of watching me dispose of my Neanderthal-noggined nemesis right before your squinty little eyes!

GREAT GASSY GOBLINS! Armageddon, *where did he go?*

CHAPTER TWO

Well, that makes thirty-*eight* times now that that sparkly toothed sponge brain has escaped my conniving clutches! I have no idea how he did it *this* time, but I am certainly man enough to place the blame squarely where it belongs.

On *you*, "dear" reader.

"Me?! But I just got here!"

EXACTLY! Things were going precisely as planned before you decided to open the book and distract me! I mean, how can I be expected to concentrate with that goofy mug of yours staring down at me all beady-eyed and everything? It's taking all the strength I can muster not to break out into hysterical laughter.

"Hey, why are you being so mean?"

Why? WHY? BECAUSE I AM VORDAK THE INCOMPREHENSIBLE, THAT'S WHY! And I am an evil Supervillain. In fact, I am the MOST EVIL evil Supervillain who has ever set foot on this or any other planet! I am also the most ~~intelagent intellijant intellugintt~~ smart! And, obviously, the handsomest. So, if you can't handle a little criticism, then perhaps you should put this book down and read something more your speed, such as:

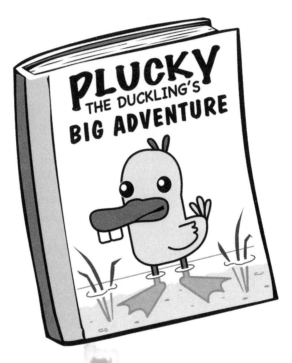

"No way! This is the most fabtastic book I have ever read! And you're right—you really are incredibly handsome!"

Well, now. That's much better.

"Hey! I didn't say that!"

Of course you did. It's right there in black ink. And the writing is even larger than usual, so you must *really* mean it.

"You wrote that yourself! And *fabtastic* isn't even a word!"

All right, look—I'm not going to sit here and argue with you. This is *MY* book and I will fill it with whatever facts I choose to make up. And you had better follow along carefully, because I will be testing you throughout the book to make sure you are paying close attention. For example:

Question #1 –
How many times has Commander Virtue escaped my conniving clutches, including today?

"Thirty-eight?"

Correct. And therein lies the problem. You see, I believe it is extremely important to keep a list of goals. I'm sure you do it yourself, although your list probably looks a little different than mine.

_____**'S**

(INSERT YOUR NAME HERE)

LIST OF GOALS

1. Remember my name without looking it up on my underwear waistband.
2. Put my shoes on the correct feet at least 50 percent of the time.
3. Make it through seventh grade before my seventeenth birthday.

Being that I am an evil Supervillain, and a brilliant one at that, my goals are far more ambitious than yours. And, unlike you, I actually have a chance to attain mine.

VORDAK THE INCOMPREHENSIBLE'S
Lip-Lickingly Loathsome List of Most Cherished Evil Goals

1. Dispose of my arch-nemesis, Commander Virtue, once and for all.
2. Take over and Rule the World.
3. Replace all the sand on the earth's beaches with Sinister Syd's Extra-Strength Itch Powder.

I change goal #3 from time to time so I don't get bored. And goals #1 and #2 used to be reversed, but I have come to realize that I cannot accomplish goal #2 without first taking care of goal #1. Case in point—just last month I was deep into my latest attempt to RULE THE WORLD by putting EVIL PLAN 1827 into action.

VORDAK THE INCOMPREHENSIBLE'S
Diabolically Brilliant Foolproof
EVIL PLAN 1827
Magnificent Moon Mayhem

STEP 1: SHOOT ROCKET WITH A SUPER-THIN EXTRA-HIGH-STRENGTH CABLE ATTACHED TO IT INTO THE SURFACE OF THE MOON.

Thoomp!

STEP 2: THREATEN TO PULL THE MOON INTO THE ATLANTIC OCEAN IF I AM NOT DECLARED THE RULER OF THE WORLD WITHIN TWENTY-FOUR HOURS.

"Hey, wait a minute. How can you be on your 1827th foolproof evil plan? If a plan is foolproof, shouldn't you only need one?"

Goofy looking *and* a smart aleck, eh? For your information, each and every one of my positively preposterous plans was utterly infallible ... as long as nothing happened that was completely out of my control. Like the sun being in my eyes. Or my alarm clock failing to go off. Or Armageddon chewing through the death ray cord.

Or—and this is the big one—Commander Virtue swooping in at the last second and thwarting me. Swooping and thwarting. Swooping and thwarting. Sometimes pouncing and foiling. But usually swooping and thwarting. ACK! Just how much can a Supervillain be expected to take?!

So, anyway, there I am—looking even more handsome than usual in my freshly cleaned costume—slowly but surely reeling that reflective orb in from space, when what happens?

Did I tell you?! If I am ever to rule this pathetic planet, I must first rid it of Commander Cowbrains.

Now, who on earth could that be, Armageddon?

Oh, hold on! I'm coming. It's a long way from the dungeon to the front door, for zounds' sake!

GREAT GASSY GOBLINS! I said I'll be right there!

WELL (HUFF), WHAT DO **YOU** WANT?

SORRY TO INTERRUPT, BUT
I'M HERE IN ANSWER TO YOUR
AD FOR AN EVIL SCIENTIST.

EVIL SCIENTIST? WHAT IN FRIGNOR'S
NAME ARE YOU BABBLING ABOUT?! I
HAVEN'T PLACED AN AD FOR ANY EVIL
SCIENTIST!

OOPS. I MUST HAVE MISCALCULATED.
MY MISTAKE. I'LL BE BACK LATER.

Well, that was odd . . . even for one of *my* books.

CHAPTER THREE

ACK! That trip up the stairs really took the wind out of me.

"You don't have an elevator in your lair?"

I did. It was a real nice one, too. It even played "Old MacDonald" through the speakers when you rode up and down in it. But that was in my old lair, the one that was destroyed by those multiheaded misfits Waxclog and Lipwartz in my last book, *Double Trouble*.

Anyway, long story short, I acquired my new lair from the Wet Nostril, who was retiring from Supervillainy to open a chain of handkerchief-laundering establishments. It's a real fixer-upper, but it *did* come with a couple of henchmen.

I call them Henchman Number One and Henchman Number Two for a number of reasons.

They are henchmen.
There are two of them.
Their real names are Bartholomew and Percival. There's no way I'm calling them *that*!
Henchman Number One is hard of hearing. Sort of like

an earmuff-wearing earthworm. He sometimes has trouble understanding my commands. Henchman Number Two possesses the eyesight of a blind trout. And they both display the intelligence of tree stumps. It's no wonder the Wet Nostril left them behind.

Ah, but what does the incompetence of my clearly clueless crew matter at this point in time? They could be the most hair-raisingly heinous henchmen in history, and I still would be unable to defeat Commander Virtue. And since I can't vanquish that golden-haired gooberhead, I have zero chance of ever Ruling the World! None. Zilch. Nada. Zippo. For as long as I have been a Supervillain, that chimp-eared champion of the people has been a huge pain in my backside!

You know that kid in school—the one who always has to one-up you? The one who, no matter how good a grade you get, gets a better one? And then rubs your face in it? The one who stars in all the school plays and captains the football team while you play the parts of "Rock Number Three" and "Tackling Dummy Number Two" respectively? The one who gets voted class president while you are elected to head up the pencil-sharpening club? The one with the perfect, blemish-free skin who calls you "Shmimple the Pimple" every time you have a breakout on your forehead? The one who gives you an atomic wedgie to the point where you can wear your underwear as a hat?

"yeah?"

THAT IS SUPPOSED TO BE ME!!! But noooooooooo—it's Commander Virtue who always gets the last laugh! Zounds, I despise that despicable do-gooder! That obnoxious namby-pamby! That prancing prima donna!

"Hey--maybe you should calm down a little."

And maybe you should clean your nasal passages with a frightened porcupine! Sure, I lose my cool every once in a while, but it's only because he haunts my every waking moment. It's like the only reason he even *became* a Superhero was to torment me. Sometimes I think if I would just hang up my cape and helmet permanently and call it quits, he would disappear altogether.

GREAT GASSY GOBLINS! THAT'S IT!

I haven't thought this completely through yet, but all I have to do to rid myself of Commander Virtue is *cease being an evil Supervillain*! It's simple, yet brilliant!

"But if you aren't an evil supervillain, how are you going to take over the world?"

Hey! I *said* I haven't thought this completely through yet.

But I *do* feel that I am on to something with this whole Commander-Virtue-not-existing idea. The problem is, my brilliant brain is so enormous that it takes a while for one of my ingenious ideas to travel from the back of my mind to the front so I can figure out what it is. And the whole process takes a lot of energy, which is making me hungry. Henchman Number One—bring me a snack. Jelly and crackers. And put it on my favorite red dish.

 WAIT. THAT LOOKS LIKE A DEAD FISH.

NO, IT'S NOT. IT'S A DEAD FISH. JUST LIKE YOU ASKED FOR.

 ACK! I SAID RED DISH! AND YOU FORGOT THE *JELLY*!

OF COURSE IT'S SMELLY. IT'S A DEAD FISH.

 WELL, WHY IN ZORGOTH'S NAME DID YOU *BRING IT HERE*?

SING IN YOUR EAR? UH . . . SURE. WHAT SONG WOULD YOU LIKE TO HEAR?

 I DON'T WANT TO HEAR ANY SONG! ZOUNDS, YOU HAVE THE EARS OF A SWEET POTATO! AND YOU'RE MAKING ME *VERY MAD, YOU LITTLE YAM!*

"MARY HAD A LITTLE LAMB"? NOT WHAT I WOULD HAVE PICKED, BUT OKAY. "MARY HAD A LITTLE LAMB, LITTLE LAMB, LITTLE LAMB . . ."

 ENOUGH ALREADY! WHAT DO YOU HAVE FOR BRAINS, ANYWAY—*CHOWDER?*

SURE, I CAN DO IT LOUDER! "MARY HAD A LITTLE LAMB, LITTLE LAMB, LITTLE LAMB . . ."

STOP! OR I'LL *CHOP OFF YOUR TONGUE!*

AT THE TOP OF MY LUNGS? *"MARY HAD A LITTLE LAMB, LITTLE LAMB, LITTLE LAMB . . ."*

 OH, FOR THE LOVE OF—

RUFF!

WHAT IS IT, ARMAGEDDON? I CAN HARDLY HEAR YOU OVER THE HORRIFIC HOWLING OF THIS HARD-OF-HEARING HENCH-TWIT!

ACK! In the midst of this deafening din, I completely forgot about your walk. We'll have to make it a quick one today, Armageddon. I have cupcakes ready to come out of the oven in fifteen minutes and we need to be back in time. Back . . . in . . . GREAT GASSY GOBLINS! THAT'S IT! *AND THIS TIME I REALLY MEAN IT!* I need to write this down while the idea is still fresh within my magnificently imaginative mind. But wait—the last time I tried to use a pencil when I was this excited, I got a wood sliver in my thumb. Quickly, Henchman Number One— cease your insufferable singing and bring me a *pencil made of metal* and some *white paper*.

 WHAT IN BLARSNOOT'S NAME IS THIS?

HANSEL AND GRETEL AND A LIGHTSABER. JUST LIKE YOU SAID.

 ZOUNDS! YOU HAVE **EARS LIKE A BAT!**

HEY, I CAN'T HELP IT IF MY REAR LOOKS FAT. I'M BREAKING IN A NEW PAIR OF HENCHMAN TROUSERS.

All right, Henchman Number Two. You're up. Get me something to write *with* and something to write *on*. And hurry! My brainstorm is beginning to fade!

Oh, for the love of . . . *That's a pretzel rod and a piece of bologna!* By the flabby fat folds of Floobar, Henchman Number Two, I've seen turnips with better eyesight than you. What does an Evil Mastermind have to do to find decent help these days?

Ah, Armageddon! I can always count on you, can't I? Okay, bring the paper and pencil here, boy. C'mon, Armageddon. No, not over there! I'm not in the mood to chase you right now, Armageddon. Bring it here! Armageddon, you are trying my patience! All right—that's it, mister. Here I come! And I'm not messing around!

Forty minutes later . . .

I told you I wasn't messing around, Armageddon. It usually takes us an hour to get to this point. Now, to put pencil to paper and record my preeminent plan.

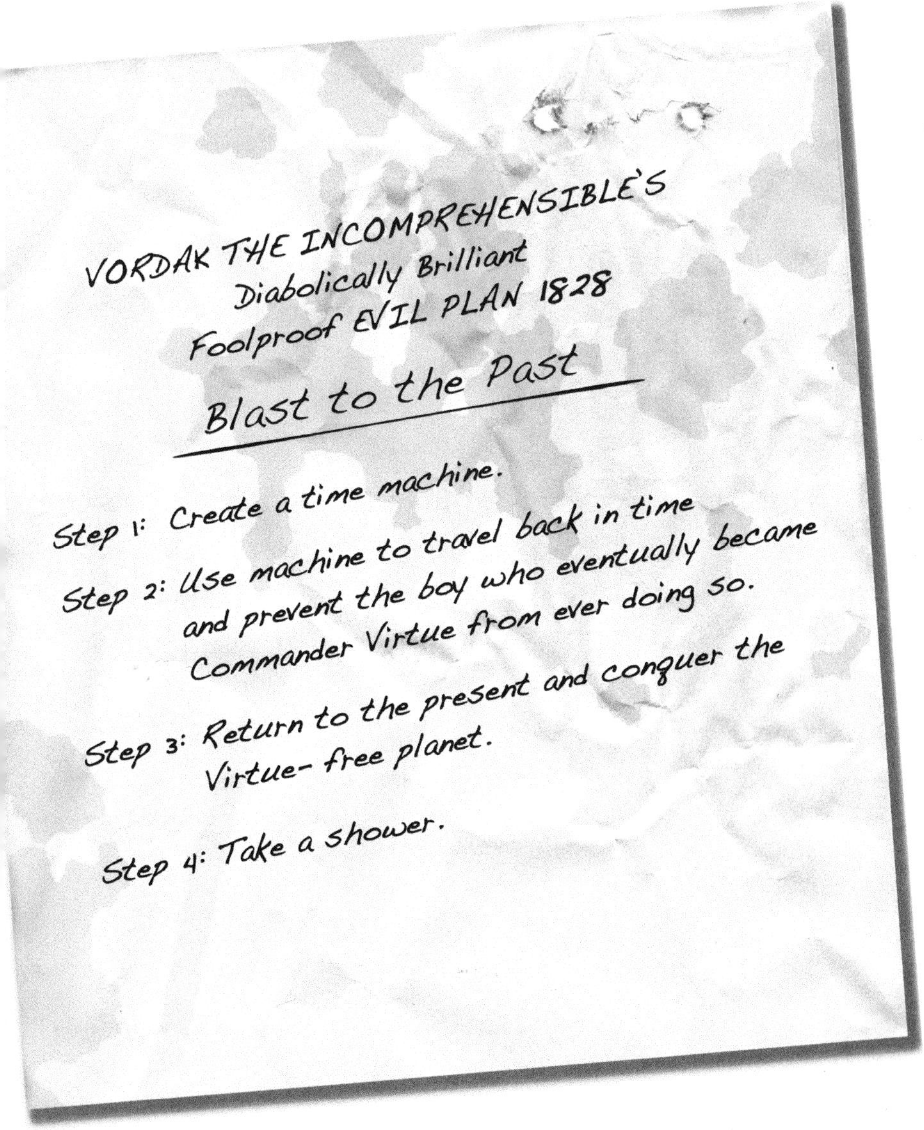

VORDAK THE INCOMPREHENSIBLE'S
Diabolically Brilliant
Foolproof EVIL PLAN 1828

Blast to the Past

Step 1: Create a time machine.

Step 2: Use machine to travel back in time and prevent the boy who eventually became Commander Virtue from ever doing so.

Step 3: Return to the present and conquer the Virtue-free planet.

Step 4: Take a shower.

MUAHAHAHAHA!!! Is that awesome, or what?

"But there's no such thing as time travel."

Of course there is, you doubting doofus. Haven't you ever heard of *The Time Machine* by H. G. Wells?

"Sure. But that's just a made-up story in a book."

I know *that*. But time travel does exist *outside* of books, too. And I'll prove it by traveling through time in *this* book.

"But how does that prove--"

SILENCE! I've put up with your birdbrained babbling up to this point because it beat having to listen to those two maddening minions of mine. But your nonstop nincompoopish negativity is beginning to nag at my nerve endings. You cannot hope to understand my brilliance because you are so clearly less intelligent than me!

"Actually, it's I."

What's you?!

"You should have said, 'You are so clearly less intelligent than I.'"

Why on earth would I say that?! I am a diabolically brilliant Evil Mastermind and you have the approximate brainpower of an asparagus stalk!

"I was talking about your grammar."

Hey! You leave that sweet old lady out of this!

Nobody talks about Gramma Incomprehensible like that! You are hereby prohibited from commenting on the events depicted within this book until such time as I deem acceptable for your return. I'm thinking probably page 59 or so. In the meantime, you can sit there quietly and watch me bask in the glow of my latest achievement in Evil Plan concoction. In fact, this one has a chance to be my best yet, as it has FOUR pulse-pounding pluses and only ONE minuscule minus.

Pulse-Pounding Pluses to My Latest Evil Plan

1. It's BRILLIANT!
2. It's SPECTACULAR!
3. Only an ABSOLUTE GENIUS could have come up with it!
4. *I* came up with it!

Minuscule Minuses to My Latest Evil Plan

1. I have no idea how to travel through time.

Now I know what you're thinking, even though I am not allowing you to say it—that seems like a pretty big minus. But I'll just do what I always do when I don't know how to do something—say the word *do* a lot. And then hire some silly-looking scientist to handle all the technical stuff. But unlike Professor Cranium and the flailing, failing Freds in my previous two books, I'll make sure it's an *evil* scientist this time.

CHAPTER FOUR

http://criminalchronicle.com/

YouTube   Twitter   Facebook   Vordak.com   Sinister Syd's   Puppy Videos

HELP WANTED

Evil scientist to assist incredibly brilliant and handsome Supervillain in his attempt to rid the world of the immensely irritating Commander Virtue. **Must be evil**. Must also be an expert in time travel. **Must also be evil**. Willingness to work for days on end in a dark, damp laboratory with no food or rest while constantly being called an imbecile is a plus. Preferred parking spot available.

Did I mention you **must be evil**?

Contact V the I, whereabouts unknown.

SUBMIT

Finished! Every word a wonder! Every period a piece of pure perfection! All I need to do now is upload this to the *Criminal Chronicle*'s website and wait for the flood of applicants to come to the door.

DING-DONG!

 UGH . . . NOT AGAIN. HENCHMAN NUMBER ONE, GO **ANSWER THE DOOR.**

DANCERS GALORE?! WHERE?

 THERE AREN'T ANY DANCERS, YOU USELESS YOKEL! NOW, **GET UP THOSE STAIRS!**

SURE, I'LL SET UP THE CHAIRS. WE WANT TO BE COMFORTABLE WHEN WE'RE WATCHING THOSE DANCERS!

 THERE AREN'T ANY—**ACK!** HENCHMAN NUMBER TWO, **YOU** CLIMB THE STAIRS AND ANSWER THE FRONT DOOR!

THERE'S STAIRS?

 OF COURSE THERE ARE, YOU NEARSIGHTED NUMBSKULL! HOW ELSE WOULD WE GET OUT OF THIS UNDERGROUND LAIR?!

THERE'S AN UNDERGROUND LAIR?!

SLAM!

Gee, what a surprise. It falls once again upon Vordak the Incomprehensible to do everything himself.

I'll bet Darth Vader doesn't have to answer his own door!

I'll bet Doctor Doom isn't saddled with a heap of helpless henchmen!

But can I get even a teensy-weensy bit of assistance from my listless assistants? Nosiree! Not old Vordak!

 YOU AGAIN?! NO ONE MAKES VORDAK THE INCOMPREHENSIBLE CLIMB THOSE STUPIDLY STEEP STEPS TWICE IN ONE DAY! PREPARE TO PLUNGE PAINFULLY INTO MY PRIZED PIRANHA PIT WHEN I ACTIVATE THAT TRAPDOOR BENEATH YOUR FEET. OH, AND COULD YOU DO ME A BIG FAVOR AND MOVE TWO FEET TO YOUR LEFT?

WAIT A MINUTE! MY NAME IS DEL . . . IRIOUS. **DOCTOR** DELIRIOUS. AND I'M HERE IN ANSWER TO YOUR AD FOR AN EVIL SCIENTIST THAT I FOUND ON THE INTERNET. SAME AS LAST TIME.

 HEY, HOW DO YOU KNOW ABOUT THAT? I HAVEN'T EVEN HAD A CHANCE TO **PUT** IT ON THE INTERNET YET. AND HOW DID YOU KNOW ABOUT IT LAST TIME YOU WERE HERE? I HADN'T EVEN **THOUGHT** OF IT YET!

BECAUSE I'M FROM THE FUTURE. I SAW YOUR HELP-WANTED AD FIVE MONTHS FROM NOW AND TRAVELED BACK IN TIME TO OFFER MY SERVICES.

WELL, WHY DID YOU SHOW UP EARLIER THIS MORNING?

THAT WAS A MISTAKE ON MY PART. I ENTERED "A.M." INSTEAD OF "P.M." ON MY TIME-CONTROL PANEL.

AH. SO YOU'RE AN INCOMPETENT CLOD. YOU SHOULD FIT RIGHT IN WITH THE REST OF MY MORONIC MINIONS.

I'LL HAVE YOU KNOW MY IQ IS 189—THAT'S BETTER THAN ALBERT EINSTEIN'S.

OH, YEAH? WELL, MINE IS 188, SO I'M ONE SMARTER THAN YOU.

ACTUALLY, HIGHER IS BETTER.

AND ACTUALLY, I MEANT TO SAY MINE IS 537. AND A HALF.

THAT'S IMPOSSIBLE! THE HIGHEST IQ EVER RECORDED IS LESS THAN HALF OF THAT.

WELL, THEN IT'S PRETTY OBVIOUS MINE WAS NEVER RECORDED, ISN'T IT? ZOUNDS, I THOUGHT YOU SAID YOU WERE SMART.

IF YOU REALLY ARE THAT INTELLIGENT, THEN WHY DO YOU NEED *MY* HELP?

BECAUSE, I'M . . . UH . . . TOO BUSY DOING *OTHER* BRILLIANT EVIL MASTERMINDISH STUFF. LIKE CREATING EVIL PLANS TO CONQUER THE WORLD! AND DEVISING SCHEMES TO ENSLAVE HUMANITY! AND TRYING TO TELL WHETHER THE LITTLE LIGHT IN MY REFRIGERATOR STAYS ON WHEN I CLOSE THE DOOR!

IT DOESN'T.

LIKE YOU WOULD KNOW. WHY ARE YOU SO INTERESTED IN HELPING ME DISPOSE OF COMMANDER VIRTUE, ANYWAY?

BECAUSE I WANT HIM GONE AS MUCH AS YOU DO.

WELL, WHY DIDN'T YOU JUST DO IT YOURSELF?

I TRIED. AND FAILED.

HA! WHAT A LOSER!

OF COURSE, I FAILED ONLY ONCE, NOT THIRTY-EIGHT TIMES.

ACK! WELL, WHY DO YOU THINK THINGS WILL BE DIFFERENT WORKING FOR ME?

LET'S JUST SAY YOU ARE UNIQUELY SUITED FOR THE JOB.

UNIQUELY SUITED? IN WHAT WAY? BESIDES BEING REALLY HANDSOME, I MEAN.

YOU'LL FIND OUT SOON ENOUGH.

OKAY, SO YOU HATE COMMANDER VIRTUE. BUT HOW DO I KNOW YOU AREN'T MAKING ALL THIS UP? HOW DO I KNOW YOU CAN ACTUALLY TRAVEL THROUGH TIME?

THINK OF A NUMBER BETWEEN ONE AND ONE TRILLION.

UM . . . OKAY.

IS IT THREE?

NOPE. IT'S 467,839,291. AND A HALF. MY LUCKY NUMBER! IT APPEARS YOU ARE A FRAUD, MY GOOFILY GOGGLED GALOOT. NOW, STEP A LITTLE CLOSER TO THE DOOR SO I CAN SLAM IT IN YOUR—

OKAY, SO YOU HATE COMMANDER VIRTUE. BUT HOW DO I KNOW YOU AREN'T MAKING ALL THIS UP? HOW DO I KNOW YOU CAN ACTUALLY TRAVEL THROUGH TIME?

THINK OF A NUMBER BETWEEN ONE AND ONE TRILLION.

UM . . . OKAY.

467,839,291.

NOT EVEN CLOSE.

AND A HALF.

GREAT GASSY GOBLINS! THAT'S RIGHT! HOW IN MORLOCK'S NAME DID YOU KNOW THAT?

EASY. THIS IS THE SECOND TIME WE'VE HAD THIS CONVERSATION. I MERELY TRAVELED BACK IN TIME AFTER YOU TOLD ME YOUR NUMBER THE FIRST TIME.

BALDERDASH! IT'S A TRICK! I'LL NEED MORE PROOF THAN THAT!

HOLD OUT YOUR RIGHT ARM.

WHAT DID THAT PROVE?

I JUST SENT YOUR ARM TEN SECONDS INTO THE PAST.

THAT'S RIDICULOUS!

CLAP YOUR HANDS.

10 SECONDS LATER...

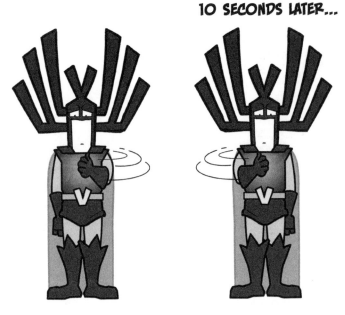

ZOUNDS! YOU REALLY HAVE MASTERED TIME TRAVEL! BUT HOW DO I KNOW THAT YOU ARE TRULY *EVIL*? LIKE MY AD SAYS—YOU *MUST* BE EVIL!

CHAPTER FIVE

All right, Delirious. Before we get started, I'm going to give you the same pep talk I give to all of my new minions— DO NOT DISAPPOINT ME IN *ANY* WAY OR IT'S SWIMMING LESSONS IN THE PIRANHA PIT FOR YOU! WITHOUT FLOATIES! I demand excellence from everyone within my organization.

THOSE TWO DON'T LOOK ALL THAT EXCELLENT.

YES, WELL, UNFORTUNATELY, I HAVE FOUND THAT THERE IS A BIG DIFFERENCE BETWEEN DEMANDING AND RECEIVING.

SO, WOULD YOU SAY THOSE TWO DISAPPOINT YOU?

 WELL, OF COURSE THEY DISAPPOINT ME! I MEAN, **LOOK** AT THEM! BRAINS OF TURNIPS. PATHETIC EYESIGHT AND HEARING. LAZY. AND THEY SMELL LIKE A PAIR OF USED GYM SOCKS LEFT IN THE BOTTOM OF A DUFFEL BAG FULL OF SICK SKUNKS. THEY ARE TOTALLY, COMPLETELY, ABSOLUTELY **USELESS** TO ME IN **EVERY** WAY.

THEN WHY HAVEN'T THEY RECEIVED SWIMMING LESSONS IN THE PIRANHA PIT?

 BECAUSE IT'S LONELY IN HERE, THAT'S WHY! THERE, I SAID IT. IT'S VERY LONELY BEING AN EVIL SUPERVILLAIN. NOBODY EVER COMES TO VISIT. THAT'S THE PROBLEM WITH LIVING INSIDE A SECRET LAIR—HARDLY ANYBODY KNOWS WHERE IT IS. AND THOSE WHO DO ARE AFRAID THEY'LL BE THROWN INTO A PIRANHA PIT OR SQUISHED BETWEEN COLLAPSING WALLS OF METALLIC SPIKES OR DROPPED INTO A VAT OF ACID OR SOMETHING. GIRL SCOUTS DON'T EVEN COME TO MY DOOR SELLING COOKIES, FOR KLORMOG'S SAKE! DO YOU HAVE ANY IDEA HOW DIFFICULT IT IS TO GO AN ENTIRE YEAR WITHOUT A SINGLE BOX OF TAGALONGS?

THANKFULLY, NO.

IS IT ANY WONDER I SO DESPERATELY DESIRE TO RID THE PLANET OF COMMANDER VIRTUE SO I CAN TAKE OVER AND RULE THE WORLD?! I'M TIRED OF HIDING AND PLOTTING AND SCHEMING. I WANT TO SIT HIGH ATOP MY THRONE SO THAT THIS PITIFUL PLANET'S PATHETIC POPULATION CAN MARVEL AT MY IMMEASURABLE MAGNIFICENCE! I WANT ALL WHO LIVE TO GAZE IN AWE AT MY HEAPS OF HEARTBREAKING HANDSOMENESS! AND I WANT ALL THE THIN MINTS I CAN STUFF DOWN MY THROAT! SO STOP YOUR WHINING, DELIRIOUS, AND LET'S GET DOWN TO THE BUSINESS OF SENDING ME BACK IN TIME!

BUT I WASN'T WHIN—

ALL YOUR BELLYACHING IS ONLY SLOWING US DOWN. I NEED TO TRAVEL BACK TO VIRTUE'S CHILDHOOD SO I CAN PREVENT HIM FROM EVER BECOMING HIS SQUARE-JAWED SELF. BUT WAIT! HOW WILL I KNOW WHICH CHILD GROWS UP TO BECOME COMMANDER VIRTUE?

EASY. I ALREADY KNO—

I WOULD HAVE TO GO BACK IN TIME AND STOP **EVERY SINGLE KID** ON THE ENTIRE PLANET FROM POSSIBLY BECOMING THAT SUPERHEROIC SAP!

NO, I CAN JUST—

ACTUALLY, NOW THAT I THINK OF IT, I WOULD ONLY HAVE TO STOP ALL THE BLOND ONES. BUT THAT'S STILL AN AWFUL LOT OF KIDS. THIS IS GOING TO BE **WAY** HARDER THAN I THOUGHT. YOU KNOW WHAT? LET'S JUST FORGET THE WHOLE THING. I MEAN, WHO SAYS I HAVE TO RULE THE WORLD, ANYWAY? THERE ARE PLENTY OF OTHER CAREERS OUT THERE FOR AN EVIL GUY LIKE ME. I COULD BECOME A SCHOOL BUS DRIVER. OR AN ORTHODONTIST. OR A NEW YORK YANKEE!

OR I COULD JUST SHOW YOU WHICH YOUNG MAN GREW UP TO BECOME COMMANDER VIRTUE! I ALREADY TOLD YOU I TRIED TO STOP HIM ONCE MYSELF AND FAILED. I KNOW WHO HE IS. OR WAS.

WELL, WHAT IN SHROOPLOR'S NAME ARE YOU WAITING FOR? TELL ME!

ACTUALLY, IT WOULD BE BETTER IF I SHOWED YOU. I LOADED A HISTORICAL SNAPSHOT DISK ON MY PAST-MASTER 3-D SLIDE VIEWER.

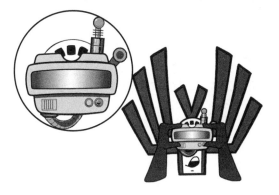

AM I SUPPOSED TO BE ABLE TO SEE SOMETHING HERE, DELIRIOUS?

HOLD ON A MINUTE. LET ME ADJUST THE FOCUS.

AGE = 1 day

BY THE WRINKLED REAR END OF RANZAR, WHAT IS THAT?!

THAT IS COMMANDER VIRTUE.

NO, IT ISN'T. COMMANDER VIRTUE IS MUCH TALLER AND HAS A FULL HEAD OF HAIR. YOU HAVE PROVEN YOURSELF TO BE WORTHLESS ALREADY, DELIRIOUS!

THAT'S COMMANDER VIRTUE **AS A BABY.**

OH. I KNEW THAT.

LET ME ZOOM OUT A BIT.

AGE = 1 day

THOSE LOOK LIKE ARMS. ZOOM OUT SOME MORE. I WANT TO SEE WHO HAS THE INTESTINAL FORTITUDE TO ACTUALLY HOLD THAT UNSIGHTLY INFANT.

AGE = 1 day

GREAT GASSY GOBLINS! IT'S MY MOM AND DAD! BUT WAIT! THAT MEANS THAT . . .

EXACTLY. COMMANDER VIRTUE JUST SO HAPPENS TO BE YOUR—

. . . MOM AND DAD VOLUNTEERED AT THE HOSPITAL TO HOLD ALL THE REALLY UGLY BABIES THAT NO ONE ELSE WANTED TO TOUCH! WHY WOULD THEY **DO** THAT?

AGE = 1 day

AND LOOK—THERE'S A YOUNG MAN DRESSED UP IN A VORDAK COSTUME. IT MUST BE HALLOWEEN. AND JUST LOOK HOW HANDSOME HE IS. IN FACT, HE'S WAY *TOO* HANDSOME TO BE AN ORDINARY CHILD. ZOUNDS, THAT'S *ME*! WHICH MEANS YOU'VE GOOFED, DELIRIOUS. THAT BABY ISN'T COMMANDER VIRTUE. IT'S MY BROTHER, KYLE.

KEEP WATCHING.

AGE = 2 years

THAT'S KYLE, ALL RIGHT. POTTY-TRAINED HIMSELF BY AGE TWO. SHOW-OFF!

AGE = 4 years

CLASSIC KYLE—HELPING MRS. PLATNORIK WITH HER GROCERIES. ALWAYS BEING HELPFUL, KIND, AND COURTEOUS. IT'S NO WONDER WE PUT HIM UP FOR ADOPTION. SPEAKING OF WHICH . . .

AGE = 5 years

AH . . . THAT MUST BE HIS NEW FAMILY. THEY APPEAR TO BE QUITE . . . WHOLESOME. KEEP IT MOVING, DELIRIOUS—I THINK I'M GOING TO BE SICK. . . .

AGE = 12 years

LOOK AT HIM! A **BOY SCOUT**, FOR CRYING OUT LOUD. HOW DID **MY** PARENTS EVER PRODUCE SOMEBODY LIKE **HIM**?

AGE = 18 years

AND THIS MUST BE HIS HIGH SCHOOL GRADUATION. HA! I'M SURE MOM AND DAD ARE GRATEFUL THEY DIDN'T HAVE TO SIT THROUGH A VALEDICTORIAN SPEECH FROM **ME**.

Okay, so this definitely proves that my parents were right to get rid of him. But regardless of how kind and thoughtful he is here, he certainly is *not* a Superhero. Commander Virtue has *superpowers*, for crying out loud. I have personally watched him crush a SpiderBot (mine!) with his bare hands. I have seen him use his laser vision to cut through a three-foot-thick steel entry door to a secret lair (mine!). And I have witnessed the results of him using his superbreath to blow out the candles on a birthday cake (mine!) from over two miles away so that the birthday boy (me!) didn't have a chance to make his wish (to RULE THE WORLD!!!).

I have read enough comic books to know that for an ordinary human like Kyle to gain the powers of someone like Commander Virtue, he would had to have been bitten by a radioactive insect. Or injected with some super-soldier serum. Or exposed to cosmic rays. So, like I said, there is *no way* Kyle ends up becoming the cretinous Commander.

KEEP WATCHING!

I stand corrected.

CHAPTER SIX

I always like to throw at least one shorter chapter into my books. So here it is. The subject of this chapter is nuclear fusion.

There. All finished.

Now you will be able to have the following conversation with your parents:

Parents: *Did you finish your reading?*
You: *Yes!*
Parents: *How much did you read?*
You: *A whole chapter!*
Parents: *Great! What was it about?*
You: *Nuclear fusion!*
Parents: *Wow! Here, have a fudge brownie!*

You can thank me later.

CHAPTER SEVEN

"Hey! We're on page 59 so I can start commenting again, right?"

Not so fast, you flatulent fathead. You must first prove that you have been following along during your banishment.

Question #2 –
What is my favorite number?

"Four hundred sixty-seven million, eight hundred thirty-nine thousand, two hundred and ninety-one."

WRONG! It appears you didn't even have the common decency to pay attention while—

"And a half."

ACK! Lucky guess. All right, I'm removing the ban on your comments. Except for the really stupid ones. Which means I probably won't be hearing from you much beyond this point.

But enough about you. It's time to get back to the interesting, awe-inspiring, *handsome* part of my story, namely **ME**. And **MY** quest to travel through time.

As we speak, Doctor Delirious is toiling away in my laboratory, working his fingers to the bone to design a time-traveling device worthy of my sensationally sinister self. It turns out the device *he* uses is a ridiculous-looking toy pig with a clock in its stomach.

Don't ask me why.

"Why?"

I JUST SAID DON'T ASK ME WHY!!

"No, I mean why can't I ask you why?"

Because I don't *know* why, that's why!

"Why wouldn't you know why I can't ask you why?"

I MEAN I DON'T KNOW WHY HE USES THE TOY PIG!

"Well, why didn't you just say so in the first place?"

WHY YOU ... *(Vordak! This is your brilliant-beyond-belief-brain speaking. Don't let this reader get under your skin. In order for your book to be successful you need readers, even rhinoceros-brained goofballs like this one. Now, take a deep breath and continue on with the story.)* **BUT I** ... *(No buts—just do it!)*

(Deep breath) Doctor Delirious uses a ridiculous-looking toy pig with a clock in its stomach to travel through time. I DON'T KNOW WHY HE CHOSE A PIG WITH A CLOCK IN ITS STOMACH! What I *do* know is that Vordak the Incomprehensible refuses to be seen parading through time while in possession of that pot-bellied porker. *That* is why Doctor Delirious is toiling away in my laboratory, working his fingers to the bone to design a time-traveling device worthy of my sensationally sinister self. And it's about time I checked in on him.

WELL?
WHAT DO YOU THINK?

I THINK IT'S A **COW** WITH A CLOCK IN ITS STOMACH.

 INDEED IT IS! I MAY HAVE OUTDONE MYSELF THIS TIME! DO YOU LIKE IT?

 DOES A DOG LIKE FLEAS?

NO.

 DOES A MOUSE LIKE SNAKES?

NO.

 DOES A CHIPMUNK LIKE WEARING LIPSTICK?

 I SUPPOSE THAT WOULD DEPEND ON THE CHIPMUNK. WHAT'S YOUR POINT?

MY POINT IS THAT **NO**—I DON'T LIKE THE LITTLE COW WITH THE CLOCK IN ITS STOMACH ANY MORE THAN I DO THE LITTLE PIG! THINK BIGGER. GRANDER! I WANT A STYLISH, DIGNIFIED TIME-TRAVELING DEVICE BEFITTING A MISCHIEVOUS MASTER OF EVIL SUCH AS MYSELF.

WHAT ABOUT A HORSE?

A HORSE! NOW YOU'RE TALKING! THAT WOULD BE A MAGNIFICENT MOUNT! GET TO WORK ON THAT IMMEDIATELY!

A horse! What a majestic mode of time transportation *that* would be! I can already see the stunned faces of astonished onlookers as I appear, as if from nowhere, astride my spectacular time-traveling stallion!

I wonder which breed Delirious will choose to create my sinister steed. An Appaloosa, maybe? A palomino, perhaps? Or will he select a sturdy Clydesdale to transport my fetching figure back to the days of Virtue's youth? Better yet—a robotic beast of glistening steel! Ah, the possibilities are endless!

HERE YOU GO!

GREAT GASSY GOBLINS! WHAT IS IT
WITH YOU AND RIDICULOUS BARNYARD
TIME-TRAVEL DEVICES?!

*SORRY, BUT IT'S THE ONLY WAY I KNOW
HOW TO MAKE THEM.*

WELL THEN, LET ME OFFER SOME
ASSISTANCE. IF YOU DON'T COME UP
WITH SOMETHING BEFITTING MY REGAL
ELEGANCE WITHIN THE NEXT TWO
HOURS, IT'S INTO THE PIRANHA PIT
WITH YOU! AND, WITH THOSE STUBBY
LITTLE ARMS OF YOURS, I HAVE A
FEELING YOU DON'T SWIM VERY WELL.
NOT THAT THAT WOULD MATTER.

One hour later . . .

At last! Delirious's time is up!

"Um . . . actually, you gave him **TWO** hours."

ACK!

*One **more** hour later . . .*

NOW Delirious's time is up! Right?

"YUP."

At last! Let's see whether he was successful.

GREAT GASSY GOBLINS! It appears my precious piranhas will have to wait at least another chapter or two before dining on our dimwittedly dressed doctor. What a magnificent machine!

It is now a simple matter of learning how it works, and I'll be off wiping Commander Virtue from existence!

WHAT DOES THIS KNOB DO?

NOTHING.

WHAT DOES THIS LEVER DO?

NOTHING.

LET ME GUESS—THE STEERING WHEEL DOESN'T TURN, EITHER.

OH, IT TURNS, ALL RIGHT.

EXCELLENT!

BUT IT ISN'T ATTACHED TO ANYTHING.

ZOUNDS, DELIRIOUS! DOES ANYTHING FUNCTION ON THIS CONFOUNDED CONTRAPTION?

A COUPLE OF BUTTONS ON THE CONTROL PANEL. BUT THIS IS MERELY THE

OUTER SHELL. I STILL NEED TO PUT THE ACTUAL TIME-TRAVEL UNIT IN IT.

WELL, HOP TO IT, YOU GOOFY-HATTED GALOOT! I DON'T HAVE ALL DAY!

 ACK! THE PIG AGAIN?! IS THIS YOUR IDEA OF A JOKE, DELIRIOUS?

I TOLD YOU BEFORE—THAT'S THE ONLY WAY I KNOW HOW TO MAKE THEM. THE REST OF THE VEHICLE IS STRICTLY FOR SHOW.

 HMMM . . . ALL SHOW AND NO SUBSTANCE. I CAN'T SAY I AM FAMILIAR WITH THE CONCEPT. NOW, HOW DOES THE BLASTED THING WORK?

I HAVE UPDATED THE DEVICE TO HOME IN ON DNA SIMILAR TO YOUR OWN. THIS WAY, THE MACHINE WILL APPEAR IN THE IMMEDIATE VICINITY OF KYLE OR ANOTHER FAMILY MEMBER, WHICH WILL SAVE YOU THE EFFORT OF SEARCHING FOR THEM. JUST SET THE DIAL ON THE PIG TO THE NUMBER OF YEARS YOU WISH TO TRAVEL INTO THE PAST, THEN PUSH THE LEAVE BUTTON. IT'S THAT SIMPLE.

BUT YOU **MUST** REMEMBER TO PUSH THE LEAVE BUTTON. IT ABSOLUTELY, POSITIVELY WILL **NOT** WORK IF YOU DON'T PUSH THE LEAVE BUTTON.

I GET IT ALREADY! PUSH THE LEAVE BUTTON. WHAT DO YOU TAKE ME FOR, DELIRIOUS, AN IGNORAMUS? WHAT ABOUT THIS RETURN BUTTON?

JUST PRESS THAT, AND YOU WILL RETURN TO THE PRESENT FROM WHENEVER IN TIME YOU HAPPEN TO BE.

AND WHAT IS THIS?

THAT'S A USB PORT FOR YOUR IPOD. AND THOSE BLACK GRILLES ON THE SIDES ARE SPEAKERS.

YES! I CAN LISTEN TO MY FAVORITE PLANET-CONQUERING TUNES WHILE I SPAN THE DECADES OF TIME!

MARY HAD A LITTLE LAMB

GREAT GASSY GOBLINS! WHO'S BEEN MESSING AROUND WITH MY IPOD?

THAT WOULD BE ME, YOUR EVILNESS. I KNOW HOW MUCH YOU LOVE THAT SONG, SO I ADDED IT TO YOUR PLAYLIST . . . AND DELETED EVERYTHING ELSE SO YOU CAN LISTEN TO IT ON AN INFINITE LOOP. NO NEED TO THANK ME.

THAT'S IT! IF I'M FORCED TO SPEND ONE MORE MINUTE WITH THESE MORONIC MINIONS, MY HANDSOME HEAD WILL SURELY EXPLODE! HOP IN, ARMAGEDDON. WE'RE HEADING BACK IN TIME AND PUTTING THIS PUTRID PRESENT BEHIND US. OR IN FRONT OF US. OR . . . OH, JUST HOP IN ALREADY!

Like heck I will! I'm not going anywhere *near* that ridiculous pigulous thingamabob! That's what lackeys are for. Henchman Number One—set the dial for minus thirty-five years.

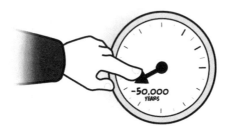

Enjoy your last few moments of existence, Commander Virtue! I am about to use every ounce of my awesomely awesome awesomeness to prevent you from ever coming into being! STAND BACK, YOU LOATHSOME LACKEYS! I AM AWAY! MUAHAHAHAHA!!!

YESSIREE! THERE'S NO TELLING HOW CRAZY THINGS MIGHT GET IN HERE ONCE THE DIMENSIONAL PORTAL HAS BEEN OPENED AND I AM HURLED DECADES INTO THE PAST ALONG THE SPACE-TIME CONTINUUM!!

THERE MIGHT BE BLACK HOLES AND VORTEXES AND ALL KINDS OF TUMULTUOUS THINGS GOING ON!!!

HOW ABOUT A LITTLE PUSH?

DELIRIOUS! YOUR FANCY-SCHMANCY TIME MACHINE *DOESN'T EVEN WORK!* AND YOU CALL YOURSELF A *GENIUS?* HA! AN ABSOLUTE AND UTTER *FAILURE* IS WHAT YOU ARE! I WOULD HAVE BEEN BETTER OFF HIRING A PRESCHOOLER TO CREATE MY TIME MACHINE! AT LEAST *SHE* WOULD HAVE BEEN POTTY-TRAINED! WELL?! WHAT DO YOU HAVE TO SAY FOR YOUR COMPLETELY PATHETIC SELF BEFORE I TOSS YOUR ODDLY PROPORTIONED BODY TO THE PIRANHAS?!

DID YOU REMEMBER TO PUSH THE LEAVE BUTTON?

OOPSIE. MY BAD.

CHAPTER EIGHT

GREAT GASSY GOBLINS! Is that a saber-toothed canary? I may not be an expert in time travel yet, but I don't recall those birds being around thirty-five years ago! That hearing-impaired hench-moron sent us back to the Stone Age! Come on, Armageddon. Let's hit the RETURN button and try this again.

NOT SO FAST. YOU HAVE TO LET THE MACHINE RECHARGE ITSELF FIRST.

 ZOUNDS! WHAT ARE *YOU* DOING HERE?

*ACTUALLY, I'M **NOT** HERE. THIS IS MERELY A HOLOGRAM OF MY HEAD. IT ALLOWS US TO COMMUNICATE BACK AND FORTH THROUGH TIME.*

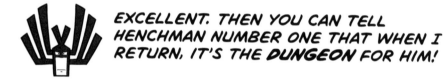

EXCELLENT. THEN YOU CAN TELL HENCHMAN NUMBER ONE THAT WHEN I RETURN, IT'S THE *DUNGEON* FOR HIM!

*HE SAYS THANKS—HE'D **LOVE** A LUNCHEON. ALTHOUGH HE WANTS TO KNOW IF THERE WILL BE BOLOGNA. HE HATES BOLOGNA.*

ACK! LOOK, JUST HOW LONG IS THIS RECHARGE GOING TO TAKE, ANYWAY?

TWO HOURS TWENTY-SEVEN MINUTES AND FORTY-ONE SECONDS. APPROXIMATELY.

 ACK!

 Well, Armageddon. It appears we're going to be here a while. I guess we may as well have a look around.

HE APPEARS TO BE THE ONE WHO THE TIME MACHINE ZEROED IN ON. HE MUST BE A DISTANT RELATIVE OF YOURS.

HA! I hardly think this prehistoric pea brain could be related to *me*. I mean, look at him! The long face. The dumpy build. And I wouldn't be caught dead putting something that ridiculous on my head.

HEY! WHO YOU?!

I AM VORDAK THE INCOMPREHENSIBLE! WHO ARE YOU?

ME BORGAK! YOU GO OR BORGAK HIT YOU WITH BORGAK HIT STICK!

HOLD ON THERE, YOU TITANIC-TOOTHED TROGLODYTE! I'M JUST PASSING THROUGH. WHAT IS GOING ON HERE?

BORGAK WANT RULE WORLD! FROM TREE WAY OVER **THERE** TO ROCK WAY OVER **THERE**! **WHOLE** WORLD!

WELL, WHO IS THAT HANGING FROM THE VINE?

THAT GRANK. HIM TRY STOP BORGAK FROM RULE WORLD. BORGAK CATCH GRANK AND DROP IN TAR.

IS THIS THE FIRST TIME YOU'VE CAPTURED HIM?

NO! THIS THIRTY-EIGHT TIME BORGAK CATCH GRANK.

WHAT HAPPENED THE OTHER THIRTY-SEVEN TIMES?

GRANK GET AWAY. BUT NOT BORGAK FAULT. SUN IN BORGAK EYES. AND BORGAK TRIP ON ROOT. AND BORGAK HENCHMEN STUPID. BUT THIS TIME BORGAK DROP GRANK IN TAR!

BY THE FOSSILIZED FEMURS OF FUMAR!
He *is* my relative!

 WELL—THIS SEEMS ODDLY FAMILIAR.

OH, WELL. MAYBE BORGAK GET GRANK NEXT TIME. BUT NOW BORGAK HUNGRY. CROG! TOG! ZOG! WE GO BACK TO CAVE. NOW!

THAT'S QUITE ALL RIGHT, YOU CULINARY CLOD. I THINK I'LL JUST . . .

 WHAT IN THE NAME OF THUNDEROUS THOOMPING IS THAT SOUND?

THAT STOMPER. BETTER RUN!

THOOMP! THOOMP! THOOMP!

 WAIT A MINUTE! I KNOW AN ELASMOTHERIUM WHEN I SEE ONE! AND THEY'RE PLANT EATERS—THEY WOULDN'T HURT A HUMAN!

OH, YEAH?! TRY TELL THAT TO ZOG.

Ouch

WE SAFE NOW. STOMPER CHASE ZOG. YOU COME IN BORGAK CAVE.

 GREAT GASSY GOBLINS! IT'S MY LAIR!!!

BORGAK LAIR!

 NO, I MEAN IT'S **MY** LAIR IN THE **FUTURE!** I'D KNOW IT ANYWHERE! THE JUTTING, TOOTH-LIKE ROCKS . . . THE SKULL-SHAPED ENTRANCE . . .

AAAAAAACK!

...THE DEEP CAVERN.

YOU EVER HEAR OF STAIRS?

NO.

 WELL, HOW DO WE GET OUT OF HERE?

USE VINE ON WALL.

 THERE'S A VINE? WELL, BY THE TANNED TOENAILS OF TARZAN, WHY DIDN'T YOU CLIMB DOWN IT INSTEAD OF FALLING LIKE I DID?!

BORGAK FIGURE PRONGHEAD MUST KNOW BETTER WAY. MUST BE MORE SMART THAN BORGAK. BORGAK WRONG.

Okay, reader. Here's the deal. I had some really impressive pictures of me using my incredible strength and agility to effortlessly climb up the vine and out of the cavern. Unfortunately, I seem to have misplaced them, so you'll just have to picture my spectacular feat in your imagination.

HA! BORGAK HAD TO *CARRY* PRONGHEAD UP VINE.

ACK! That's only because my gloves were too slippery! And I was still dizzy from the fall! And the sun was in my eyes! None of that matters, however. My time machine is now fully recharged, so it's time to go. But before I do—Borgak, you can't go around being carried on a log by a couple of nitwitted Neanderthals if you ever hope to Rule the World. So I made you something.

It's called a *wheel*, and it will allow you to travel faster and over greater distances than ever before. With a tool such as this at your disposal, there is no limit to what you might accomplish on this prehistoric planet.

And now I must return to my own time. Come on, Armageddon. Let's go.

CHAPTER NINE

 ALL RIGHT, HENCHMAN NUMBER ONE— GIVE ME ONE GOOD REASON WHY I SHOULDN'T THROW YOU INTO THE PIRANHA PIT THIS INSTANT!

WELL, AN INSTANT IS A VERY SHORT PERIOD OF TIME SO, STRICTLY SPEAKING, YOU'RE ALREADY TOO LATE. NOW, IF YOU HAD SAID *"THIS MINUTE,"* WE MIGHT HAVE HAD TIME TO HURRY OVER TO THE PIT SO YOU COULD TOSS ME IN. OR BETTER YET, YOU COULD HAVE BEEN LESS SPECIFIC AND SAID *"LATER THIS EVENING"* OR *"TOMORROW"* OR—

 OH, SO **NOW** YOU CAN HEAR ME!

WHAT?

 SO NOW YOU CAN HEAR ME!

HUH?

I SAID: "SO NOW YOU CAN HEAR ME!"

YOU'LL HAVE TO SPEAK UP. I DON'T KNOW IF YOU'RE AWARE OF THIS, BUT I'M A LITTLE HARD OF HEARING.

ACK! If I could reach my hair under this helmet, I'd be pulling it out right now! All right, Henchman Number Two, this is your chance to impress me and move up a rung on the henchman ladder. Set the time dial to minus thirty-five years.

RIGHT AWAY, YOUR SUPERVILLAINESS.

 **WHAT** DID YOU CALL ME?

YOUR SUPERVILLAINESS. YOU KNOW, LIKE "YOUR IMMENSENESS" OR "YOUR EVILNESS." I THOUGHT IF I STARTED SHOWING YOU A LITTLE MORE RESPECT IT WOULD HELP ME MOVE UP THAT LADDER.

 WELL, IT MAKES ME SOUND LIKE A **FEMALE** SUPERVILLAIN, YOU CONTEMPTIBLE CLOD.

WAIT. YOU'RE **NOT**?

 ACK! DO I **LOOK** LIKE A WOMAN TO YOU?!

I DON'T KNOW. YOU'RE JUST SORT OF A BLURRY BLOB.

WELL, DO I *SOUND* LIKE A WOMAN?!

YUP. MY AUNT EDNA. ONLY HER VOICE WAS DEEPER. SAME SORT OF NASAL QUALITY, THOUGH.

Okay—I need to calm down before my brain fluid begins to boil! The Wet Nostril will pay dearly for saddling me with that pair of pea-brained parameciums. But that is for another day. I must focus all my evil energy on the task at hand—stopping Kyle from ever becoming Commander Virtue. Unfortunately, my time machine still requires another two hours to recharge before I can travel back to his childhood. There is nothing to do but wait.

'Wait? For two hours? What am I supposed to do for all that time?"

Well, you *could* stare at my glorious visage on the cover. It would surely take at *least* two hours to soak up every fabulous feature, every delectable detail of my stunningly sensational self!

"That sounds boring."

Boring?! I'll have you know I stare at myself in the mirror every day for hours on end and have never once become *bored*. I mean, just *look* at me, for Moorflog's sake! All right, I'll tell you what—if you promise not to bother me so much as one single time during the next chapter, I will show you my two-step plan to pass two hours of time.

"Really? Okay. I promise."

VORDAK THE INCOMPREHENSIBLE'S
Two-Step Plan to Pass Two Hours of Time

1. Stare at the back of your hand for one hour and fifty-three minutes.

2. Read the poem on the next page.

"Hey! That's not an exciting plan at all!"

Well, it's not my fault the back of your horrid little hand is so uninteresting. Besides, where in the name of the plan do I ever say it's going to be exciting? Anyway, don't fret. I wrote the poem myself, so you can rest assured you will be treated to one positively priceless piece of poetry! You may begin staring at your hand . . . *now*. I'm going to take a nap.

One hour and fifty-three minutes later . . .

Yaaawwwnnnnn! Well, *that* was refreshing. Here's your poem:

GOOD EVIL HELP IS HARD TO FIND

Good evil help is hard to find.
Too many *dolts*—and I'm being kind.
One time I tried to Rule the School.
I needed help, and got a fool.
His name? Professor Cranium.
Had the brains of a geranium.
That head of his was huge in size
Which made him seem extremely wise.
But, truthfully, his brain was small.
He couldn't help me out at all.
Freeze-ray creation was his task.
Did he succeed? No need to ask.
When he was finished with his ray
It wouldn't freeze an ice-cube tray.

Another time, as is well known,
I needed help to make a clone.
I hired two guys. Their names were Fred.
And they were clones, is what they said.
I brought them in so I could see
If they could clone a younger me.
But things got quickly out of hand.
Their numbers started to expand.
Instead of two Freds, there were four.
Soon after that, there were five more.
What did these Freds provide when done?
Nine times more stupidness than one.

And now I have two henchmen who
Are surely no more bright than you.
One barely hears; one barely sees.
And both have brains of cottage cheese.
That's right—those two are nincompoops.
I ask for cakes; they bring me soups.
I call them Henchman One and Two.
I give them simple tasks to do.
But still they struggle, still they strain.
They're slowly driving me insane.
But I must keep them, right or wrong
Till something better comes along.

ACK! You read it too fast! You were supposed to recite
it slowly and savor every sensational snippet! Now, we
still need to kill a bit more time, so here's a little beauty
I wrote back when I was eleven years old:

I WANNA PIRANHA

I wanna piranha
I wannit right now
I wanna piranha
I wannit and how

I wanna piranha
To show all my friends
I wanna piranha
To bite their rear ends

I wanna piranha
To put in my tank
I wanna piranha
To munch my friend Frank

I wanna piranha
That's angry and mean
I wanna piranha
To chew on colleen

Colleen

I wanna piranha
With really sharp teeth
I wanna piranha
To nibble on Keith

Raoul

I wanna piranha
That's feisty and cruel
I wanna piranha
To chomp on Raoul

I wanna piranha
But noticed a trend
When I got my piranha
I lost all my friends

There. That did it. The device is completely recharged and ready to go! Henchman Number Two—did you set the time dial to minus thirty-five years?

NOT YET, YOUR EXTREMELY IMPRESSIVENESS.

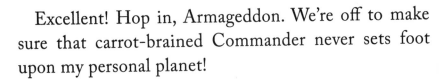

ALL SET!

Excellent! Hop in, Armageddon. We're off to make sure that carrot-brained Commander never sets foot upon my personal planet!

CHAPTER TEN

Well, Armageddon, I don't see any tar pits. Or Elasmotheriums. Or dimwitted cave dwellers with poor grammar. It appears Henchman Number Two overcame his complete lack of functioning brain cells and actually sent us back to the correct year!

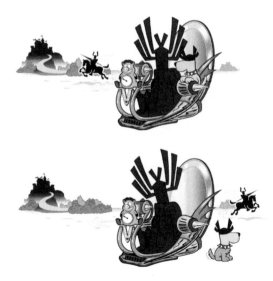

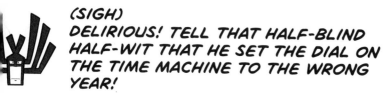 (SIGH)
DELIRIOUS! TELL THAT HALF-BLIND HALF-WIT THAT HE SET THE DIAL ON THE TIME MACHINE TO THE WRONG YEAR!

SURE THING.
HE SAYS, "THERE'S A TIME MACHINE?"

 ACK! WHEN I GET BACK THERE, DELIRIOUS, YOU WILL SET THE DIAL ON THAT RIDICULOUS PIG OF YOURS!

SORRY. NO CAN DO. THE SUPERVILLAIN-HENCHMEN RULE BOOK PROHIBITS IT.

THE SUPERVILLAIN-HENCHMEN RULE BOOK? WHAT IN GRAKZOR'S NAME IS THAT?

 ANY SUPERVILLAIN WHO EMPLOYS HENCHMEN AGREES TO ABIDE BY THE BOOK'S RULES OF CONDUCT. AND RULE 17 SPECIFICALLY STATES THAT A HENCHMAN, AND ONLY A HENCHMAN, IS ALLOWED TO OPERATE TIME-TRAVEL DATE-SETTING MACHINERY.

 ACK! AND WHAT IF I DECIDE TO IGNORE THIS RIDICULOUS BOOK OF RULES?

*ACCORDING TO RULE 32, YOU WILL HAVE TO ANSWER TO A GENTLEMAN NAMED MR. M. AND, ACCORDING TO RULE 33, YOU DEFINITELY DON'T WANT **THAT** TO HAPPEN.*

WELL, WHAT IF I WERE TO TOSS THE HENCHMEN INTO THE PIRANHA PIT?

THERE DOESN'T APPEAR TO BE A RULE AGAINST THAT.

Excellent! So now I simply need to wait two hours twenty-seven minutes and forty-one seconds before I can return home and deal with those lunkheaded lackeys. Slightly less at this point. I wonder what year this *is*, anyway.

-850 YEARS

MINUS 850 YEARS! GREAT GASSY GOBLINS, ARMAGEDDON! THAT MEANS WE'VE LANDED SOMEWHERE AROUND (LET'S SEE . . . SUBTRACT 5 . . . CARRY THE 1 . . . CHANGE THE 2 TO A . . .) 220 AD!

ACTUALLY, IT'S MORE LIKE 1160 AD.

OH, LOOK—MR. SMARTY-PANTS
HAS A CALCULATOR. BIG DEAL. I DID
MY CALCULATION IN MY *HEAD*, AND
YOU HAVE TO ADMIT—I WAS PRETTY
DARNED CLOSE.

OU WERE OFF BY MORE THAN 900 YEARS!

BAH. A MERE ROUNDING ERROR.
WHAT'S THE DIFFERENCE BETWEEN 220
AD AND 1160 AD, ANYWAY? NEITHER ONE
HAD CHEEZ DOODLES. BUT ENOUGH OF
THIS NONSENSE. DELIRIOUS! WHO
IS THAT ON THE HORSE?

IT APPEARS TO BE A KNIGHT.

WELL, OF COURSE IT'S A KNIGHT, YOU
HOLOGRAPHIC HALF-WIT! BUT *WHO* IS
HE?

HE WAS THE CLOSEST ONE TO THE TIME
MACHINE WHEN IT APPEARED, SO HE MUST
BE RELATED TO YOU. BEYOND THAT, I HAVE
NO IDEA. WHY DON'T YOU JUST ASK HIM?

"WHY DON'T YOU JUST ASK HIM?"
WERE YOUR HEAD NOT A HOLOGRAM,
DELIRIOUS, I WOULD POKE YOU IN THE
EYE RIGHT NOW!

 EXCUSE ME, SIR KNIGHT, BUT WHO ARE YOU?

 I BE MORLAK! AND WHOEST BE THOU?

 I BE-ETH VORDAK THE INCOMPREHENSIBLE. AND THERE IS A PRETTY GOOD CHANCE THAT YOU ARE MY GREAT-GREAT-GREAT-GREAT-GREAT-GREAT-GREAT-GREAT-GREAT-GREAT-GRANDFATHER—ONLY ADD ABOUT TWENTY-FIVE MORE "GREAT"S IN THERE.

SAYETH WHAT?! I FEELETH NOT THAT OLD!

 WHAT I MEAN TO SAY IS I HAVE TRAVELED HERE FROM THE FUTURE.

AH. I HATH NO IDEA WHAT THAT DOST MEAN.

I COME FROM A TIME THAT DOESN'T EXIST YET. UNDERSTAND?

NOPETH.

USING HIGHLY ADVANCED TECHNOLOGY, I HAVE CREATED A CROSS-DIMENSIONAL PORTAL, WHICH HAS ENABLED ME TO MANIPULATE THE SPACE-TIME CONTINUUM, THUS ALLOWING ME TO EXIST HERE, NINE HUNDRED YEARS PRIOR TO MY OWN BIRTH.

WELL, WHY DIDST THOU NOT JUST SAYETH SO? IT DOTH APPEAR THAT PEOPLE IN THE FUTURE BE-ETH NONE TOO BRIGHT.

WHY DO YOU SAY THAT?

THINE ARMOR WOULDST STOP NEITHER SWORD NOR ARROW. AND THINE HELMET LOOKETH QUITE STUPID.

YOU SHOULD TALK!

ACKETH!

WHAT ARE YOU DOING OUT HERE RIDING BACK AND FORTH WITH THAT SWORD, ANYWAY?

LOOSENING UPETH. I DOST INTEND TO STORM YON CASTLE.

STORM THE CASTLE? BUT YOU DON'T HAVE AN ARMY.

OF COURSETH I DO.

GREAT GASSY GOBLINS!

WHERE?! WHERE BE THOSE VILE GREEN CREATURES WHO DOTH FARTETH SO LOUDLY?!

RELAX. IT'S JUST A FIGURE OF SPEECH. I SAY IT WHEN SOMETHING SHOCKS OR AMAZES ME. THERE ARE NO SUCH THINGS.

LIKE HECKETH THERE AREN'T! MANY A NIGHT HATH I BEEN RUDELY AWAKENED BY THE SOUND AND SMELL OF YON FOUL BEASTS AS THEY SNEAKETH INTO MINE HOME AND CUTTETH THE CHEESE! TRULY, THEIR TORMENT OF ME BE NEVER-ENDING!

ZOUNDS! I ALWAYS WONDERED WHERE OUR FAMILY CAME UP WITH THAT PHRASE! BUT ENOUGH ABOUT THOSE PINT-SIZE POLLUTERS—WHY IN LORGON'S NAME ARE YOU TRYING TO STORM A CASTLE WITH ONLY THREE PEOPLE?

BECAUSE WE WOULDST LOOK QUITE FOOLISH STORMING A HUT. BESIDESETH, IF EVER I AM TO RULETH THE WORLD, I DOTH REQUIRE YON CASTLE FOR MINE EVIL LAIR.

BUT THE CASTLE IS SURROUNDED BY A MOAT AND ITS WALLS ARE LINED WITH ARCHERS.

MINE ARMOR SHALT PROTECTETH ME FROM THE STING OF THEIR ARROWS.

BUT WON'T YOU SINK TRYING TO CROSS THE MOAT IN YOUR ARMOR?

BAH! 'TIS SIMPLE! I SHALT SHED MINE ARMOR AND SWIMMETH CROSS YON MOAT.

 THEN WHAT ABOUT THE ARROWS?

 BAH! 'TIS SIMPLE! I WILT DON MINE ARMOR TO PROTECTETH ME FROM THE STING OF THEIR ARROWS!

 OH, FOR THE LOVE OF . . . **ARE YOU BEGINNING TO SEE THE PROBLEM HERE?**

 VERILY, I AM! WHAT IF I NEEDST GO TO THE BATHROOM WHILST IN MINE ARMOR?! I DIDST, AFTER ALL, CHUCKETH DOWN A BEANETH BURRITO FOR LUNCH.

 ACK! LOOKETH—I MEAN **LOOK**—WHY DON'T YOU JUST USE THAT CATAPULT OVER THERE TO LAUNCH ROCKS AT THE CASTLE?

 DOES YOUR CATAPULT WORK?

OF COURSETH IT DOES! WHY WOULDST I HAVE A CATAPULT THAT DIDST NOT WORK?

 WELL THEN, WHAT ARE WE WAITING FOR? HAVE YOUR . . . UM . . . ARMY LAUNCH A FEW ROCKS AT THE CASTLE!

FWOOSH!

THWAP!

SLICE!

Oucheth

I THOUGHT YOU SAID YOUR CATAPULT WORKED?

THAT IS NOT MY CATAPULT.

ACK! WELL, WHERE IS **YOUR** CATAPULT?

'TIS HITHER!

HITHER?

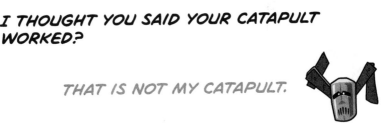

NO, NOT **THITHER!** HITHER! BE-EST THOU BLIND, FOR GLORNAKETH SAKE?

I **SAID** HITHER, YOU IRON-CLAD CLOD! PERHAPS YOUR HELMET IS ON TOO TIGHT!

AT LEAST I KNOWETH THE DIFFERENCE BETWIXT HITHER AND THITHER!

 ACK! DELIRIOUS, WHAT IN YORVATH'S NAME IS HE YAKKING ABOUT?!

HE'S SPEAKING MIDDLE ENGLISH. *HITHER* MEANS "HERE" AND *THITHER* MEANS "THERE."

AH! MORLAK—I SEE WHAT THE PROBLEM IS HITHER. LET ME COME OVER THITHER TO **YOUR** CATAPULT SO WE MAY BEGIN LAUNCHING ROCKS AT THE CASTLE.

WHY IS THERE A PILE OF ROCKS HALFWAY BETWEEN US AND THE CASTLE?

THOU SHALT FINDETH OUT SOON ENOUGH.

 **WELL, YOU OBVIOUSLY NEED TO MOVE CLOSER.**

VERILY WE HAVE TRIED. BUT MINE ARMY BE NOT PLEASED WITH THE RESULTS.

All right, look, Morlak. I like you. Well, maybe not *like*, but I certainly *respect* you. Actually, that's not true, either. Let's face it—you're a complete ignoramus and I am embarrassed to have you as an ancestor. But you *are* family, so I feel it's my duty to help you out, hither.

My time machine is now fully recharged, so it's time to go. But before I do—Morlak, you can't go around catapulting rocks halfway toward a castle if you ever hope to Rule the World. So I made you something.

It's called a *cannon* and it will allow you to launch projectiles over far greater distances than you ever thought possible. With a tool such as this at your disposal, there is no limit to what you might accomplish on this medieval mess of a planet!

And now I must return to my own time. Come on, Armageddon. Let's go.

CHAPTER ELEVEN

Zounds, Armageddon! Traveling through time is enough to make even the handsomest evil super genius thirsty! His dog, too, I'll bet. Henchman Number Two! Fetch Armageddon a bowl of water.

HERE YOU GO, BOY!

AND HENCHMAN NUMBER ONE—BRING ME
A **CHERRY COKE!**

 NO, NOT A **SCARY POKE!**

 NO, NOT A **BURIED BLOKE.**

 NO, NOT SOME MERRY FOLK! YOU MISERABLE MELON HEAD! FOR AS LONG AS YOU'VE BEEN HERE, YOU HAVEN'T DONE AS I'VE ASKED EVEN ONCE! AND THE SAD THING IS YOU AREN'T EVEN MY WORST HENCHMAN!

I'll tell you, Armageddon—this dimwitted duo is living proof that two wrongs don't make a right. . . . *Or do they?!* By the balding butt cheeks of Brapnorak— *that's it*!

"What's it?"

I knew my brilliance would leap to the fore at some point! You see, the problem is that I've been having those meatheaded minions work separately.

"So?"

Soooo . . . they are absolutely, positively, without question the *worst* henchmen in the *history* of henchmaning. A pair of tree stumps would do a better job. Now, hold on to your hat, because here comes the really brilliant part! I, Vordak the Incomprehensible, will—

"wait a second. I'll be right back."

What? *Why?*

"I need to find my hat. So I can hold on to it."

That was a figure of speech, you literal lunkhead! It means that what I have to say is of such mind-blowing brilliance that you need to prepare yourself so you aren't bowled over when you hear it!

"oh. well, I found my hat, anyway, so is it all right if I just go ahead and hold on to it?"

Oh, go ahead. Now, as I was saying—I, Vordak the Incomprehensible (even now I have a hard time believing what a brilliant plan this is!), will have my two henchmen *work together*! That way they will cancel each other out and actually do what I want them to do!

"Wait--**That's** your 'brilliant' plan? You made me search all over to find my Commander Virtue hat just so you could tell me you're going to have them work together?"

For the last time—I didn't tell you to go look for your doggone Commander Virtue hat! That was a figure of... *WAIT A MINUTE!* You have a **Commander Virtue** hat?

"Sure. He's my favorite."

WHAT?! I thought *I* was your favorite!

"Nope."

I don't believe it! If I'm not your favorite, then why are you reading MY book?!

"Because--commander virtue is in it."

ACK! And here I thought maybe you were different. I thought maybe you wouldn't fall for all that "Truth and Justice" baloney. I thought maybe you could actually relate to my struggles against a Superhero who has been given all the advantages in life. What is it about that slack-jawed Super*zero* that you find so to your liking, anyway?!

"well, he's superstrong. And he can fly. And he always beats his arch-nemesis. And his costume looks really cool. He's awesome!"

Oh, yeah?! I have all that, too! I mean, except for the superstrength. And the flying. And the arch-nemesis beating. But I DO have a super-cool costume!

"where, in your closet?"

Very funny! I'll have you know that every prized piece of my applause-worthy apparel is primo-cool.

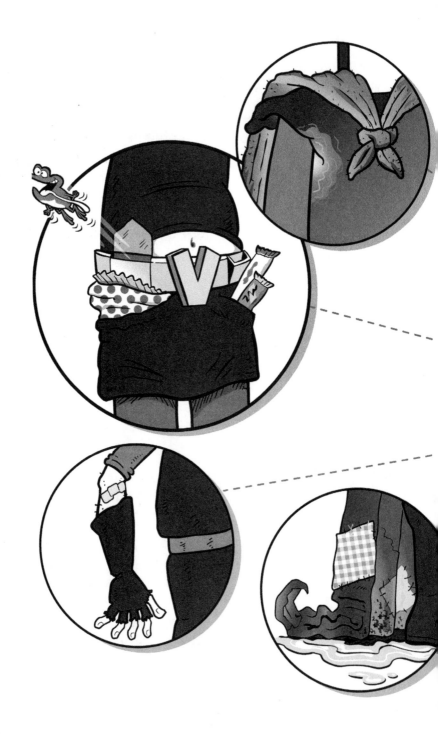

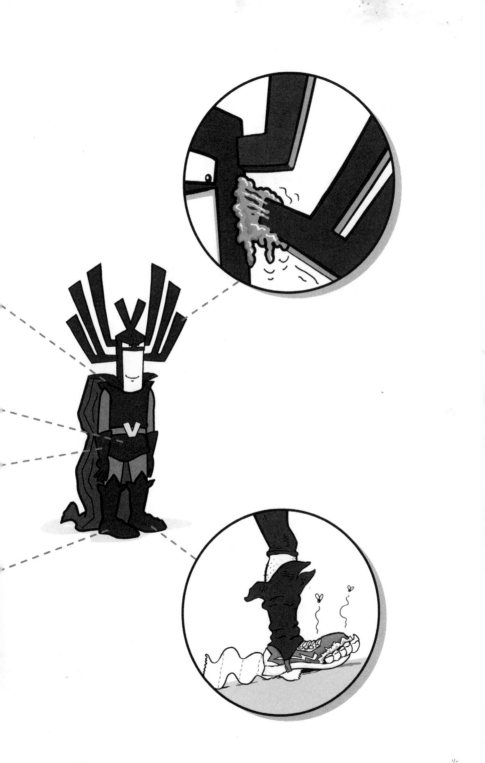

And I have an evil lair! And a SpiderBot! And a piranha pit! Plus, I am WAY more handsome than that square-headed Sasquatch.

"Then why do you wear a helmet?"

Because it's *awesome*, that's why! The mere sight of its blackened blades has been known to reduce even the mightiest of world leaders to pathetic piles of murbling mush!

"Is *murbling* even a word?"

Of course it is! It's the adjective form of the verb *murble*, as in *"Just look at that mighty world leader murble. Can you murble any more, Mr. murble boy? Murble murble murble!"* But enough about murbling. Because of your terrible taste in role models, it appears that I will have to settle for being your favorite Super*villain*.

"Um, actually . . ."

Oh, come *ON*, now!!

" . . . that would be the Blue Buzzard."

SERIOUSLY?! That bulbous-beaked blowhard?! What can he do that I can't do at least a hundred times better?!

"Eat hot dogs. Like when he beat you in that hot-dog-eating contest in your last book."

Hey! That was a *team* hot-dog-eating contest! And my teammate was positively pathetic! Besides, the sun was in my eyes! And the ketchup was too spicy! And I had a big breakfast that morning! And . . . ACK!!! You have wasted nearly an entire chapter with your relentless rambling! Now I have only a few pages remaining in which to board my time machine and prevent Commander Virtue from coming into being! I'd better write smaller. Now—where are those two incompetent clods?

RIGHT HERE, YOUR HEINOUS HIGHNESS.

ALL RIGHT—I GIVE UP. WHAT IN THE NAME OF THOMAS EDISON ARE YOU TWO UP TO NOW?

WE WERE IN THE MIDDLE OF TRYING TO CHANGE THE LIGHTBULB IN THE HENCHMEN'S BATHROOM WHEN YOU CALLED FOR US.

WHY DIDN'T YOU JUST USE THE *ADJUSTABLE LADDER*?

YOU'RE DARN RIGHT I WAS READY TO BUST MY FULL BLADDER! WHY DO YOU THINK I WAS TRYING TO CHANGE THE LIGHTBULB?

(SIGH.) WELL, WHY DO YOU STILL HAVE THE BULB IN YOUR HAND?

IT WAS PITCH-DARK IN THE BATHROOM. WE COULDN'T FIND THE SOCKET TO SCREW THE NEW BULB INTO.

 **HOW ABOUT USING THE FLASHLIGHT?**

I'M PRETTY SURE THE FLASHLIGHT WON'T SCREW INTO A LIGHT SOCKET.

GREAT GASSY GOBLINS! I MEANT HOW ABOUT USING THE FLASHLIGHT TO FIND THE LIGHT SOCKET IN THE BATHROOM!

NO CAN DO. WE CAN'T FIND THE FLASHLIGHT.

WHY NOT?

WE KEEP IT IN THE BATHROOM.

ACK! Do you know I can actually *feel* my brain cells detaching themselves from my frontal lobes and escaping down my nasal passages to avoid being subjected to this dimwitted drivel any longer?! Armageddon—hop in and let's be on our way while I still have enough wits about me to push the LEAVE button!

And now to put my ingenious henchmen-teamwork plan into effect! First, I will order Henchman Number One to tell Henchman Number Two to set the time dial to minus thirty-five years. Henchman Number One will undoubtedly give Henchman Number Two the wrong setting. But Henchman Number Two will undoubtedly set the dial to something other than what he was told by Henchman Number One! Therefore, it follows that I will be sent back in time exactly thirty-five years, just as I intended! It's foolproof! And once I arrive at my historic destination, I shall prevent my fiendish family from giving young Kyle up for adoption, thereby ensuring that—

EXCUSE ME, BUT COULD YOU SPEED IT UP A BIT? I STILL NEED TO USE THE BATHROOM.

VERY WELL. HENCHMAN NUMBER ONE— TELL HENCHMAN NUMBER TWO TO SET THE TIME DIAL TO MINUS THIRTY-FIVE YEARS!

WHY DON'T I JUST DO IT MYSELF?!

BECAUSE, YOU SONICALLY STUNTED SIMPLETON, THE LAST TIME I GAVE YOU THAT RESPONSIBILITY I WAS NEARLY TRAMPLED BY A PREHISTORIC RHINOCEROS! NOW, STOP QUESTIONING MY SUPREME INTELLECT AND JUST PASS THE MESSAGE ALONG TO HENCHMAN NUMBER TWO.

WHATEVER. HENCHMAN NUMBER TWO—SET THE TIME DIAL TO PLUS TWO HUNDRED YEARS.

SURE THING. THERE. YOU'RE GOOD TO GO!

YES! My ingenious plan has worked to perfection! Hang on, Armageddon! Next stop, 1978! *Nothing can stop me now!* MUAHAHAHAHA!!! MUAHAHAHAHA!!!

CHAPTER TWELVE

Two hours twenty-seven minutes and forty-one seconds later . . .

WOW, THAT WAS FAST!

YOU SET THE DIAL TO TWO HUNDRED YEARS INTO THE FUTURE, YOU DISMAL DUNDERHEAD!

WELL, ISN'T THAT WHAT YOU WANTED?

OF COURSE NOT! I WANTED TO TRAVEL THIRTY-FIVE YEARS INTO THE PAST!

THEN WHY DIDN'T YOU SAY THAT?

BECAUSE, THE LAST TIME I TOLD YOU WHERE I **REALLY** WANTED TO GO, I ENDED UP CATAPULTING ROCKS AT A MEDIEVAL CASTLE!

BUT HOW WOULD THAT HELP YOU STOP KYLE FROM BECOMING COMMANDER VIRTUE?

IT WOULDN'T!

OKAY. NOW YOU LOST ME.

THAT'S IT! AS MUCH AS I AM SICKENED BY THE THOUGHT OF TOUCHING THAT REPULSIVE PORCELAIN PIG, I WILL SET THE TIME DIAL **MYSELF!**

SORRY, PAL, BUT ONLY A HENCHMAN CAN OPERATE THE PIG. DEM'S DA RULES.

WHO ARE YOU AND WHAT ARE YOU DOING HERE?

YOU CAN CALL ME MR. M. YOUR HENCHMEN SAID YOU MIGHT TRY PULLIN' SOMETHIN' LIKE THIS, SO THEY GAVE ME A CALL.

I DON'T KNOW HOW YOU GOT IN HERE, BUT NOBODY TELLS VORDAK THE INCOMPREHENSIBLE WHAT HE CAN AND CANNOT DO WITHIN THE BOWELS OF HIS OWN EVIL LAIR! AND I INTEND TO SET THAT PIG! WHO'S GOING TO STOP ME?!

MY ASSOCIATE.

 ZOUNDS! HOW DID I NOT SEE **HIM** BEFORE?

YOU KNOW THE DRILL. AS LONG AS YOU HAVE HENCHMEN WORKING FOR YOU, THEY'RE THE ONLY ONES WHO CAN SET STOMACH-MOUNTED TIME-TRAVEL DIALS.

 WELL, THAT DECIDES IT, THEN. THE TIME HAS COME TO DISPOSE OF THOSE INCOMPETENT CLODS IN THE PIRANHA PIT!

NOT SO FAST THERE, BUB. HENCHMEN CAN ONLY BE THROWN INTO A PIRANHA PIT ON THE THIRD TUESDAY OF EACH MONTH. DEM'S DA RULES.

 ACK! BUT THAT'S NEARLY THREE WEEKS FROM NOW! VERY WELL, THEN—I'LL JUST TOSS THEM INTO MY ACID VAT AND BE DONE WITH IT.

SORRY, CHUM. ACID VATS CAN ONLY BE USED FOR HENCHMAN DISPOSAL ON WEEKENDS. DEM'S DA RULES.

WELL, WHAT IN VOSHNOOT'S NAME CAN I DO TO GET RID OF THEM TODAY?!

LEMME CHECK. ACCORDING TO THE RULE BOOK, YOU *CAN* SHRINK THEM DOWN TO THE SIZE OF DUST MITES.

EXCELLENT!

BUT, TECHNICALLY, THEY'D STILL *BE* HERE, SO . . .

SO I'M OUT OF OPTIONS.

YOU COULD ALWAYS BECOME A HENCHMAN YOURSELF.

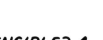

VORDAK THE INCOMPREHENSIBLE? A HENCHMAN?! SURELY YOU JEST!

I NEVER JEST.

YES. I CAN SEE THAT. SO—BE MY OWN HENCHMAN, EH? PERHAPS YOU'RE ON TO SOMETHING THERE. AFTER ALL, I HAVE NEVER HAD A **BRILLIANT** HENCHMAN BEFORE. OR ONE OF SUCH IMMENSE HANDSOMENESS. NOT TO MENTION I WOULD ALWAYS BE THERE WHEN I NEEDED ME. ALL RIGHT—I HAVE MADE UP MY MIND! I'LL DO IT! AND ONCE VORDAK THE INCOMPREHENSIBLE MAKES UP HIS MIND, **THERE IS NOTHING IN THE KNOWN OR UNKNOWN UNIVERSE THAT CAN CHANGE IT!**

GREAT. JUST SIGN HERE ON THE DOTTED LINE AND I'LL HAVE A BLACK TURTLENECK AND WOOL CAP SENT RIGHT OVER.

WHAT?! I'VE CHANGED MY MIND. TURTLENECKS DON'T COMPLEMENT MY FIGURE. SO IT LOOKS LIKE MY TIME-TRAVELING PLANS ARE DOOMED AND I AM FOREVER CURSED TO HAVE COMMANDER VIRTUE THWARTING MY EVERY EVIL MOVE! AND ALL BECAUSE I'M STUCK WITH A COUPLE OF HALF-WITTED HENCHMEN WHO CAN'T SEE OR HEAR OR, MOST IMPORTANTLY, THINK WELL ENOUGH TO SET A SIMPLE TIME-TRAVEL DIAL! LET'S GO, GENTLEMEN. I'LL WALK YOU TO THE DOOR.

DON'T YOU THINK THAT IF IT WAS THAT EASY, A BRILLIANTLY EVIL GENIUS SUCH AS MYSELF WOULD HAVE THOUGHT OF IT ALREADY?

I MEAN, I WOULD HAVE TO BE A COMPLETE ANVILHEAD TO GIVE UP ON MY ENTIRE EVIL PLAN WHEN SUCH A SIMPLE SOLUTION EXISTED.

CHAPTER THIRTEEN

All right, you incompetent clods—listen up! I refuse to allow your lack of functioning brain bits to prevent me from accomplishing the task at hand. Henchman Number Two—bring me a pretzel and a piece of bologna!

Great Gassy Goblins! It worked. I may just be enough of a genius to pull this off!

Henchman Number One,
Set the dial in the pig's stomach to -35 years.
NOW!
MUAHAHAHAHA!!!

-Vordak

 HENCHMAN NUMBER ONE—*TAKE THIS NOTE!*

BAKE WHAT GOAT?

 HERE!

AHHHHH. GOTCHA, BOSS.

 DELIRIOUS! CHECK HENCHMAN NUMBER ONE'S SETTING ON THE DIAL. I WANT NO MISTAKES THIS TIME!

YOU KNOW, IF YOU WOULD HAVE ASKED ME TO CHECK THE SETTINGS ON THE OTHER TRIPS, YOU COULD HAVE AVOIDED ALL YOUR PREVIOUS FAILURES.

 *NOW* YOU TELL ME! ZOUNDS, DELIRIOUS, WHY DIDN'T YOU MENTION THAT EARLIER?! I CAN'T BE EXPECTED TO THINK OF EVERYTHING!

WELL, I JUST ASSUMED YOU KNEW WHAT YOU WERE DOING, WHAT WITH ALL THE BRAGGING ABOUT YOUR BRILLIANCE AND SO FORTH.

 YADDA YADDA YADDA. JUST LET ME KNOW WHEN THIS INFERNAL CONTRAPTION IS READY TO GO!

OH, IT'S READY NOW.

EXCELLENT! LET'S GO,
ARMAGEDDON!

WHAT'S THE MATTER, BOY? DON'T YOU
WANT TO GO FOR A RIDE?

I'LL LET YOU STICK YOUR HEAD OUT OF
THE CROSS-DIMENSIONAL TIME-VORTEX
WINDOW!

And now, Commander Virtue, prepare yourself to not exist! This time I will not fail! Although, if I do, I have already made up a list of excuses why. In fact, just to play it safe, I think I'll save my "MUAHAHAHAHA"s for after we appear successfully back in 1978.

CHAPTER FOURTEEN

Let's see . . . no cockeyed cavemen . . . no nincompoopish knights . . . no futuristic flying cars. So far, so good! Let's take a look around.

Why, that looks just like my childhood home! And that looks just like my childhood tree! And by the bruised big toe of Burplar, that looks just like my childhood me! GREAT GASSY GOBLINS! Armageddon, that *is* me! And that means I have finally done it! I have traveled back in time to my childhood, and I did it almost single-handedly!

WHAT DO YOU MEAN "ALMOST SINGLE-HANDEDLY"?

WELL, I DID END UP USING BOTH HANDS FOR A LITTLE WHILE THERE.

YOU SEEM TO HAVE FORGOTTEN THAT IT'S MY TIME MACHINE YOU'RE USING.

AND YOU SEEM TO HAVE FORGOTTEN THAT I CAN TURN YOU INTO A PIRANHA TREAT! SURE, YOU MIGHT HAVE DESIGNED THE SILLY TECHNOLOGY STUFF THAT ACTUALLY ALLOWS ME TO TRAVEL ACROSS INFINITE TIME-SPACE DIMENSIONS, BUT THE COOL CHAIR-VEHICLE THINGY WAS MY IDEA! AND DON'T YOU FORGET IT!

ACTUALLY, I DESIGNED AND BUILT THAT, TOO.

BECAUSE I TOLD YOU TO! THERE IS NOTHING MORE PATHETIC THAN SOMEONE TRYING TO TAKE CREDIT FOR SOMEONE ELSE'S ACCOMPLISHMENTS! NOW, PIPE DOWN. IT'S TIME FOR ME TO CONFRONT MY YOUNGER ME.

SORRY, I'M NOT SUPPOSED TO TALK TO STRANGERS.

 STRANGERS?! DON'T YOU KNOW WHO I AM?

I'VE NEVER SEEN YOU BEFORE IN MY LIFE.

 OF COURSE YOU HAVE—EVERY SINGLE DAY IN THE MIRROR! DOESN'T THIS HELMET LOOK FAMILIAR? THE CAPE? THE BOOTS? THE UTILITY BELT?

NOT REALLY.

IT'S YOU! I MEAN, IT'S ME!
I MEAN, YOU'RE ME BEFORE I BECAME
ME. I MEAN, I'M **YOU** AFTER YOU
GREW UP FROM **YOU** TO BECOME **ME**!
ISN'T IT OBVIOUS?!

LOOK, YOU'RE GOING TO HAVE TO LEAVE,
WHOEVER YOU ARE. I HAVE A POEM I NEED
TO FINISH FOR ENGLISH CLASS TOMORROW
AND I'M STUCK ON A LINE.

LET ME SEE THAT.

I WANNA PIRANHA

I wanna piranha
I wannit right now
I wanna piranha
I wannit and how

I wanna piranha
To show all my friends
I wanna piranha

TO BITE THEIR REAR ENDS.

EXCUSE ME?

THE NEXT LINE. IT'S "TO BITE THEIR REAR ENDS."

HEY, THAT'S NOT BAD.

 NOT BAD? IT'S BRILLIANT! UNFORTUNATELY, MS. CHORFSKY WOULDN'T KNOW BRILLIANCE IF IT JUMPED UP AND BIT HER ON THE CHEEK MOLE.

HEY, MS. CHORFSKY IS MY ENGLISH TEACHER! HOW DID YOU KNOW THAT? HAVE YOU BEEN FOLLOWING ME?

 OF COURSE NOT! MS. CHORFSKY WAS MY TEACHER, TOO. AND YOU'RE GOING TO GET A D-PLUS ON THAT POEM.

HOW DO YOU KNOW THAT?

BECAUSE THAT'S WHAT I GOT ON IT. I WROTE THE POEM, TURNED IT IN, AND SHE GAVE ME A D-PLUS. I'M JUST WARNING YOU SO YOU AREN'T AS DISAPPOINTED AS I WAS.

WHO ARE YOU?

I'M YOU, VORDAK THE INCOMPREHENSIBLE! LONG STORY SHORT, I'M TRYING TO RULE THE WORLD, RIGHT? BUT I KEEP GETTING THWARTED BY COMMANDER VIRTUE. IT TURNS OUT THAT YOUR BROTHER, KYLE, IS PUT UP FOR ADOPTION BY MOM AND DAD, AFTER WHICH HE LANDS IN A WONDERFUL HOME AND IS BITTEN BY A RADIOACTIVE INSECT, INJECTED WITH SUPER-SOLDIER SERUM, AND EXPOSED TO COSMIC RAYS THAT, NATURALLY, TURN HIM INTO COMMANDER VIRTUE, WHO I CANNOT DEFEAT. SO I TRAVELED BACK IN TIME TO CONVINCE MOM AND DAD TO KEEP KYLE SO HE NEVER BECOMES COMMANDER VIRTUE IN THE FIRST PLACE. GOT IT?

OF COURSE. WHY DIDN'T YOU JUST SAY THAT IN THE FIRST PLACE? HEY, WHO'S THAT WITH YOU?

OH, THAT'S JUST ARMAGEDDON AND DOCTOR DELIRIOUS. ONE IS CONSTANTLY DROOLING AND SCRATCHING AND RUBBING HIS REAR END ON THE GROUND. AND THE OTHER ONE IS MY DOG.

BA-DUM

TSSSHHH!

NOW, LIKE I SAID, WE NEED TO MAKE SURE MOM AND DAD **DO NOT** PUT KYLE UP FOR ADOPTION! COME WITH ME.

DING-
DONG!

YEAH, YEAH. WHAT IS IT?

 HI, MOM! HI, DAD! YOU'LL NEVER BELIEVE IT! IT'S ME, VORDAK!

OH, WE KNOW WHO YOU ARE, PUMPKIN. HOW NICE OF YOU TO STOP BY AGAIN!

 AGAIN? BUT I JUST GOT HERE!

DON'T TELL ME—YOU TRAVELED HERE FROM THE FUTURE IN ORDER TO CONVINCE US NOT TO PUT LITTLE KYLE HERE UP FOR ADOPTION BECAUSE HE'LL TURN INTO A SUPERHERO AND FOIL ALL YOUR FUTURE ATTEMPTS TO RULE THE WORLD.

 UH . . . YEAH. BUT HOW DID YOU KNOW—

 SON, THIS IS THE THIRD TIME IN THE LAST THREE DAYS THAT YOU'VE SHOWN UP ON OUR DOORSTEP, AND IT'S ALWAYS THE SAME THING. I'LL TELL YOU WHAT I TOLD YOU THE OTHER TWO TIMES—IF IT MAKES YOUR LIFE EASIER, THEN SURE, WE'LL HANG ON TO KYLE. NOW, WE REALLY NEED YOU TO STOP REAPPEARING IN OUR TIME LIKE THIS. ONE VORDAK IS MORE THAN ENOUGH FOR YOUR MOM TO KEEP TRACK OF.

YOU REALLY ARE QUITE THE HANDFUL, YOU KNOW. BYE-BYE NOW, SWEETIE! NAVIGATE THE INTERDIMENSIONAL WORMHOLES CAREFULLY!

ARE WE REALLY GOING TO KEEP KYLE?

NO, BUT IT WAS THE ONLY WAY I COULD GET HIM TO LEAVE.

CHAPTER FIFTEEN

 WELL, **THAT** WAS ODD. I DON'T REMEMBER BEING HERE ANY OTHER TIMES. HAVE **YOU** SEEN ME HERE BEFORE?

NO. BUT I'M USUALLY IN CLASS OR SERVING DETENTION OR CAUSING GENERAL CHAOS THROUGHOUT THE NEIGHBORHOOD, SO I'M NOT AROUND A LOT.

 DELIRIOUS—WHAT IS THE MEANING OF THIS?

OH, I COULD EXPLAIN IT TO YOU, BUT I'M SURE YOU'D RATHER FIGURE IT OUT **SINGLE-HANDEDLY.**

 ACK!

HEY! I LIKE THAT WORD! ACK! I'M GOING TO START USING IT WHENEVER I'M FRUSTRATED OR ANNOYED.

 IT STOPS BEING FUN QUICKLY. TRUST ME.

Now to figure out what's going on here. I will use my masterful command of deductive logic to determine exactly what is happening. First the facts. We know that I have now traveled back to this time period three separate times. We also know that I don't remember the other two. And lastly, in all three visits, my father promised not to put Kyle up for adoption.

Okay, give me a minute to sort through this. I must allow my magnificent mind time to sort through the data, compute all the possibilities, and come up with the only possible answer.

A few more seconds should do it. . . . The answer is beginning to reveal itself within the boundaries of my bombastically brilliant brain tissue. . . . I almost have it. . . . Almost . . . Almost . . . GOT IT! The answer is obvious! There must be THREE Kyles!

WELL . . . THIS IS DEPRESSING.

 WHAT? THAT WE NOW HAVE TO DEAL WITH THREE KYLES INSTEAD OF ONE?

NO. THAT I'M GOING TO BE A COMPLETE IGNORAMUS WHEN I GROW UP.

 ACK! AND I SUPPOSE **YOU** COULD DO BETTER?!

I'M GUESSING A BOWLING BALL COULD DO BETTER.

 ACK! ACK! ACK! DID YOU FORGET WHO YOU'RE TALKING TO?!

UNFORTUNATELY, NO. AND YOU'RE RIGHT— THOSE "ACK"S HAVE **ALREADY** STOPPED BEING FUN. LOOK, HERE'S WHAT MUST HAVE HAPPENED. YOU SHOWED UP HERE TODAY AND DAD PROMISED NOT TO PUT KYLE UP FOR ADOPTION. THINKING YOUR PLAN WAS SUCCESSFUL, YOU WENT BACK TO YOUR OWN TIME ONLY TO DISCOVER THAT COMMANDER VIRTUE WAS STILL THERE. MEANING THEY REALLY **DID** GET RID OF KYLE. SO YOU CAME BACK HERE, BUT A DAY EARLIER THIS TIME. YOU TALKED TO MOM AND DAD AGAIN, AND DAD AGREED TO KEEP KYLE . . . AGAIN.

YOU ONCE AGAIN TRAVELED BACK TO YOUR OWN TIME AND FOUND THAT COMMANDER VIRTUE WAS **STILL** THERE. SO YOU CAME BACK HERE YET A **THIRD** TIME TWO DAYS AGO, AND EVERYTHING REPEATED AGAIN.

ZOUNDS! I DON'T REMEMBER BEING SUCH AN UNWIELDY WINDBAG! BUT THAT **WOULD** EXPLAIN WHY DAD SAID I HAD SEEN HIM THREE DAYS IN A ROW. LET'S PUT YOUR THEORY TO THE TEST. DELIRIOUS! BEFORE I WASTE MY TIME COMING BACK HERE, I NEED TO KNOW IF COMMANDER VIRTUE STILL EXISTS IN OUR TIME. HAVE HENCHMAN NUMBER ONE WARM UP THE DEATH RAY.

YUP. HE'S STILL HERE.

DRAT! YOUNG ME WAS RIGHT! MOM AND DAD HAVE NO INTENTION OF KEEPING KYLE, NO MATTER WHAT THEY TELL ME. I CAN'T SAY THAT I BLAME THEM, EITHER. HIS KINDNESS AND PERKINESS AND CARING NATURE ARE SIMPLY TOO HORRIBLE TO BE AROUND. I MUST THINK OF ANOTHER WAY, BUT WHAT?

WELL, YOUR PARENTS ARE GOING TO PUT HIM UP FOR ADOPTION BECAUSE HE'S *NICE.* SO IT ONLY SEEMS LOGICAL THAT THEY *WOULDN'T* PUT HIM UP FOR ADOPTION IF HE WAS—

A *TALKING GIRAFFE!* THAT'S IT! IF KYLE WERE A TALKING GIRAFFE, HE WOULD BE FAR TOO VALUABLE TO GIVE UP!

UH . . . ACTUALLY, THAT'S NOT WHAT I WAS GOING TO SAY.

GOOD, BECAUSE I HAVE NO IDEA HOW TO TURN HIM INTO A *REGULAR* GIRAFFE, MUCH LESS ONE THAT CAN TALK.

AS I WAS SAYING, THEY WOULDN'T GET RID OF KYLE IF HE WAS—

ABLE TO TURN CORNFLAKES INTO GOLD!

NO.

MADE OF JELLY BEANS?

NO.

SUPERGLUED TO THEIR KNEECAPS?

SERIOUSLY?

WELL WHAT, THEN?! I'VE JUST ABOUT RUN OUT OF FANTABULOUS IDEAS HERE!

NOT NICE! IF YOUR PARENTS ARE GOING TO PUT HIM UP FOR ADOPTION BECAUSE HE'S NICE, IT ONLY SEEMS LOGICAL THAT THEY WOULDN'T PUT HIM UP FOR ADOPTION IF HE WAS NOT NICE. IF HE WAS EVIL.

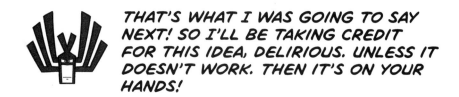

THAT'S WHAT I WAS GOING TO SAY NEXT! SO I'LL BE TAKING CREDIT FOR THIS IDEA, DELIRIOUS. UNLESS IT DOESN'T WORK. THEN IT'S ON YOUR HANDS!

So I need to turn Kyle evil. It's times like this that I wish I still had my Villainous Vorcuum.

"Villainous vorcuum? What's that?"

Well, well. And where have you been? Not to say I haven't enjoyed your absence.

"I've been trying to keep up with all this time-travel stuff. It's pretty confusing, you know."

Bah! A piece of tree bark would be confusing to you. If you had read my last book, *Double Trouble*, you would know *exactly* what a Villainous Vorcuum is. I had my cloning scientists, the Freds, create it for me.

It was a dazzlingly diabolical device designed to suck all the goodness out of a person. I tested it out on a nice little fellow named Delbert with spectacular results!

Too spectacular, in fact.

Anyway, once the Vorcuum had served its purpose, I had it converted into something that was a bit more useful around the lair.

So that's why, as I said earlier, I wish I still had it.

"Wow. Thanks for the explanation. But how come you spent so much time describing something you don't even have anymore?"

I have no idea. It just seemed like the right thing to do.

CHAPTER SIXTEEN

So that's it, then. I have to find some way to turn Kyle evil.

Okay. That's just not going to happen. I'd have a better chance of sneaking up on a Valtroonian Snow Beast than I would turning that adorable adoptee-to-be into a bristling bundle of evil.

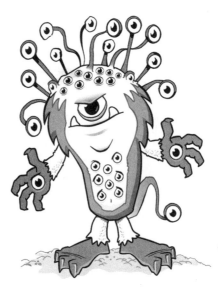

It is once again time to put my magnificent mind to work and come up with an alternate plan.

Must . . . concentrate.
Must . . . focus.
Must . . . find an aspirin. . . . All this focusing and concentrating is giving me a headache!

ACK! It's no use! I have done too much brilliant thinking already today. Even *my* brain has its limits. Delirious—you seem to be quite the smarty-pants. Any suggestions?

WELL, HE DOESN'T NECESSARILY HAVE TO *BE* EVIL. YOU JUST NEED YOUR PARENTS TO *THINK* HE IS.

YES! THAT'S IT! STARTING FROM SCRATCH, I SHALL CREATE A HIGHLY ADVANCED NEUROLOGICAL HELMET THAT, WITH THE AID OF A STATE-OF-THE-ART NUCLEAR-POWERED COMPUTER MAINFRAME, WILL DOWNLOAD FALSE MEMORIES OF KYLE BEING EVIL INTO MY PARENTS' BRAIN TISSUE! SURE, IT WILL TAKE YEARS, IF NOT DECADES, TO COMPLETE, BUT THE END RESULT WILL BE WELL WORTH THE WAIT! MUAHAHAHAHA!!!

ACTUALLY, I WAS THINKING MORE ALONG THE LINES OF HAVING YOUR YOUNGER SELF BREAK A VASE OR TWO AND BLAME IT ON KYLE.

 HMM. I SUPPOSE THAT COULD WORK AS WELL. ALL RIGHT, WE'LL GO WITH YOUR PLAN—UNDER ONE CONDITION.

WHAT'S THAT?

THAT WE CALL IT *MY PLAN.*

FINE.

OKAY, YOUNGER ME. LISTEN CAREFULLY. HERE'S WHAT YOU NEED TO DO—

I'M STANDING RIGHT HERE! I ALREADY HEARD DOCTOR DELIRIOUS EXPLAIN HIS PLAN.

 MY PLAN! IT'S *MY PLAN!* AND I CAN PROVE IT!

VORDAK THE INCOMPREHENSIBLE'S
Diabolically Brilliant
Foolproof EVIL PLAN 1829
Blatant Brother Blame

Step 1: Have my younger self break a vase
or two and blame it on Kyle.

NOW, GET A MOVE ON. WE NEED TO CONVINCE MOM AND DAD THAT KYLE'S A BAD KID WITHIN THE NEXT TWO HOURS. SPONGEBOB SQUAREPANTS IS ON AT EIGHT O'CLOCK BACK HOME AND MY DVR IS BROKEN SO I CAN'T RECORD IT.

YOU KNOW, I'M NOT SURE I REALLY WANT TO DO THIS. I MEAN, IF IT WORKS, I'M GOING TO BE STUCK LIVING WITH THAT GOOFY GOODY TWO-SHOES FOR THE NEXT TEN YEARS!

LOOK, IS RULING THE WORLD YOUR MAIN GOAL IN YOUR LIFE OR NOT?

YOU KNOW IT IS!

THEN WHAT IN FNAFNEER'S NAME ARE YOU WAITING FOR?!

TWO WHOLE HOURS WASTED DOING AWFUL THINGS THAT I DIDN'T EVEN GET CREDIT FOR. I SURE HOPE RULING THE WORLD IS WORTH IT.

HOW DO YOU THINK *I* FEEL? I NOW HAVE THE MEMORIES OF EVERYTHING YOU JUST DID, AND I HAVE HAD TO LIVE WITH THEM FOR THE PAST THIRTY-FIVE YEARS! BUT IT WILL ALL HAVE BEEN WORTHWHILE IF THE RESULT IS A WORLD FREE OF COMMANDER VIRTUE! DELIRIOUS! HAVE HENCHMAN NUMBER ONE WARM UP THE DEATH RAY ONCE AGAIN!

SORRY, BUT HE'S STILL DANGLING FROM THE FLAGPOLE.

WOW! THAT IS ONE IMPRESSIVE PAIR OF UNDERWEAR! ALL RIGHT, THEN. HAVE HENCHMAN NUMBER TWO DO IT.

OKAY. THE RAY HAS BEEN TURNED ON. NO SIGN OF COMMANDER VIRTUE. HENCHMAN NUMBER TWO APPEARS QUITE RELIEVED. APPARENTLY, HE'S WEARING REALLY OLD UNDIES.

GREAT GASSY GOBLINS! ARMAGEDDON, I FINALLY DID IT! *I RID THE WORLD OF COMMANDER VIRTUE!*

CHAPTER SEVENTEEN

 GREAT GASSY GOBLINS, DELIRIOUS! WHAT IS *THIS*?!

A CAGE.

 I CAN SEE THAT, YOU BESPECTACLED BIRDBRAIN! I MEAN, WHAT AM I DOING *INSIDE* OF IT?!

YOU APPEAR TO JUST BE SITTING THERE, HELPLESSLY IMPRISONED.

 IMPRISONED? BY WHO?

BY AN EVIL GENIUS OF SUCH DIABOLICAL FIENDISHNESS THAT THERE IS NO ONE ON THIS ENTIRE PLANET CAPABLE OF CHALLENGING HIS AWESOME MAGNIFICENCE!

I IMPRISONED **MYSELF?**

OF COURSE NOT, YOU GARBLING GASBAG! **I** DID!

HEY! WATCH THE NAME-CALLING, YOU LUNKHEADED LETTUCE-BRAIN! AND WHAT DO YOU MEAN **YOU** DID? YOU'RE NO DIABOLICALLY FIENDISH EVIL GENIUS. YOU'RE JUST **YOU**, AN UNIMPORTANT TIME-TRAVEL SCIENTIST WITH A VERY ODDLY SHAPED BODY.

HA! THAT'S WHAT I LED YOU TO BELIEVE, BUT I AM ACTUALLY FAR MORE MENACING THAN I APPEAR!

WELL, THAT'S NOT SAYING MUCH.

GO AHEAD—HAVE YOUR FUN. BUT **YOU** ARE THE ONE BLABBERING AWAY FROM WITHIN THE CONFINES OF THAT STEEL CAGE. AND NOW THAT I HAVE YOUR ATTENTION, IT'S TIME YOU KNOW THAT THE BRILLIANT VILLAIN WHO PUT YOU THERE IS **NOT** DR. DELIRIOUS AT ALL, BUT RATHER . . .

TA-DAH!

A NEARSIGHTED ELF WITH A BAD HAIRCUT? I DON'T GET IT.

IT'S ME, YOU HILARIOUSLY HELMETED HAMMERHEAD! DELBERT!

AGAIN WITH THE NAME-CALLING. DIDN'T YOUR PARENTS TEACH YOU TO RESPECT YOUR ELDERS?

SURE. BUT THAT WAS BEFORE YOU SUCKED ALL THE GOODNESS OUT OF ME WITH YOUR VORCUUM. REMEMBER?

WELL, OF COURSE I REMEMBER! THAT VORCUUM WAS ONE OF THE MOST BRILLIANTLY SINISTER INVENTIONS OF MY INCOMPARABLE CAREER!

AND IT APPEARS TO HAVE WORKED TO PERFECTION, BECAUSE YOU SEEM LIKE QUITE THE VILLAINOUS VARMINT. NOW, LET ME OUT OF HERE!

LET YOU OUT? BUT I'VE JUST NOW CAPTURED YOU! AND, WITH BOTH YOU **AND** COMMANDER VIRTUE OUT OF THE WAY, **THERE IS NO ONE TO STOP ME FROM CONQUERING AND RULING THE ENTIRE PLANET!** BWAHAHAHAHA!!!

ALL RIGHT—HOLD ON A SECOND THERE. AS I RECALL, OUR DEAL WAS THAT WE WOULD WORK **TOGETHER** TO RID THE WORLD OF COMMANDER VIRTUE.

WE DID.

AND THEN **I** WOULD CONQUER AND RULE THE PLANET WHILE YOU TRIPPED AND FELL ACCIDENTALLY INTO MY PIRANHA PIT. IT'S A PRETTY STANDARD SUPERVILLAIN-LACKEY AGREEMENT.

WELL, I AM NOT EXACTLY YOUR STANDARD LACKEY, NOW, AM I? NO—IT IS I, **DELBERT,** WHO SHALL RULE THE WORLD WHILE YOU, VORDAK, SPEND THE REMAINDER OF YOUR DAYS IN THAT PATHETIC LITTLE CAGE.

AH, BIG DEAL.

WITHOUT ANY CHEEZ DOODLES!
BWAHAHAHAHA!!!

WHAT?!?! OKAY! A COUPLE OF THINGS,
HERE. FIRST OFF—IT'S "MUAHAHAHAHA!!!"
NOT "BWAHAHAHAHA!!!" YOU SOUND LIKE
A SICK GOAT. AND, SECONDLY—OH, YEAH?!

KLANK!

DRAT!! MISSED!!

CLICK!
CLICK!
CLICK!
CLICK!
CLICK!

KLANK!

DRAT! DRAT! DRAT! DRAT! DRAT! DRAT!

NICE TRY, YOU HIDEOUSLY HELMETED HAS-BEEN. AND NOW I'M OFF TO RULE THE WORLD. SEE YOU LATER, YOU INCOMPREHENSIBLE CLODHOPPER!

 NOT SO FAST! YOU STILL HAVE MY HENCHMAN TO DEAL WITH!

AS I WAS SAYING—THERE IS NO ONE LEFT TO STOP ME!

GREAT GASSY GOBLINS! YOU'RE HERE! NOW! IN THE PRESENT! IT CANNOT BE! I GAVE YOU ALL THE CREDIT FOR BREAKING THAT LAMP AND DOING ALL THAT OTHER BAD STUFF! MOM AND DAD WERE SO PROUD! THERE WAS NO WAY THEY WOULD HAVE GOTTEN RID OF YOU!

DON'T BE RIDICULOUS. I GLUED THAT LAMP BACK TOGETHER AGAIN THAT EVENING. AND I CLEANED UP ALL THAT OTHER STUFF, TOO. I WAS PUT UP FOR ADOPTION THE VERY NEXT DAY. IT ALL WORKED OUT FOR THE BEST, THOUGH. I WAS ADOPTED BY A WONDERFUL, SHARING, CARING FAMILY.

BUT I HAD HENCHMAN NUMBER TWO ACTIVATE THE DEATH RAY! IF YOU WERE STILL AROUND, WHY DIDN'T YOU SWOOP IN AND THWART HIM, LIKE YOU DID HENCHMAN NUMBER ONE?

OH, I WAS ON MY WAY. BUT WHEN I GOT CLOSER, I SAW THAT HE HAD IT AIMED DIRECTLY AT YOUR OWN EVIL LAIR. SO I FIGURED, WHY BOTHER?

OOPSIE.

 ACK! SO, COMMANDER VIRTUE—OR SHOULD I SAY "KYLE"—YOU'VE KNOWN ALL ALONG THAT I WAS YOUR BROTHER?

OF COURSE.

 AND YOU NEVER TOLD ME, EVEN WHEN I CAPTURED YOU ALL THOSE TIMES AND PLACED YOU INTO MY DIABOLICALLY CLEVER YET EXTREMELY SLOW-ACTING DEATH TRAPS AND YOU KNEW THE END WAS NEAR.

WELL, THE END WASN'T *THAT* NEAR. I ALWAYS KNEW I COULD ESCAPE, USUALLY BECAUSE OF SOMETHING STUPID YOU WOULD DO. SO I LET YOU CAPTURE ME FROM TIME TO TIME. HEY, YOU'RE MY BROTHER AND I WANTED YOU TO FEEL GOOD ABOUT YOURSELF.

ACK! WELL, YOU MUSCLE-BOUND MUTTONHEAD—BROTHER OR NOT, I *WILL* USE THE IMMEASURABLE MAGNITUDE OF MY MAGNIFICENT MIND TO ULTIMATELY DEFEAT YOU! AND I *WILL* EVENTUALLY RULE THE WORLD! AND THERE IS *NOTHING* YOU CAN DO TO STOP ME! DO YOU HEAR ME?! NOTHING! MUAHAHAHAHA!!!

VORDAK THE INCOMPREHENSIBLE is a world-class Supervillain and the Evil Master of all he surveys. His first three books, *Vordak the Incomprehensible: How to Grow Up and Rule the World*, *Rule the School*, and *Double Trouble* have inspired a whole new generation of minions and fiends. His current whereabouts are unknown. You are hereby instructed to visit Vordak online at www.vordak.com, and he will know if you don't, so beware.

About the Minions

Scott Seegert was selected to transcribe Vordak's notes based on his ability to be easily captured. He has completely forgotten what fresh air smells like and has learned to subsist on a diet of beetles, shackle rust, and scabs. As far as he knows, he still has a wife and three children in southeast Michigan.

John Martin had the great misfortune of being chosen by Vordak to illustrate this book. He hasn't seen the sun in years and spends his free time counting down the months to his annual change of underwear. The last he heard, he also had a wife and three children living in southeast Michigan.

GREAT GASSY GOBLINS!
Your collection of the immortal works of

VORDAk
THE INCOMPReHENSIBLe

is not COMPLETE?
Vordak commands you to buy ALL the
books in the series!